P9-DGV-364

$13.95

Waon. M.S. (book review)

1990-91

THE SHADOW WARRIOR

THE SHADOW WARRIOR

PAT ZETTNER

Atheneum   1990   New York

WASHINGTON MIDDLE SCHOOL LIBRARY
Olympia, Washington

For my good friends from SAWG

Copyright © 1990 by Pat Zettner

All rights reserved. No part of this book may be reproduced
or transmitted in any form or by any means, electronic or
mechanical, including photocopying, recording, or by any
information storage and retrieval system, without permission
in writing from the publisher.

Atheneum
Macmillan Publishing Company
866 Third Avenue, New York, NY 10022
Collier Macmillan Canada, Inc.
First Edition
Printed in the United States of America
Designed by Nancy Williams
10 9 8 7 6 5 4 3 2 1
Library of Congress Cataloging-in-Publication Data
Zettner, Pat.
The shadow warrior/by Pat Zettner.—1st ed. p. cm.
Summary: When underlords burn her home, a young Solgant embarks on
a dangerous mission to find her brother, aided by two enemies of her
people, a Danturin goblin and an Eodan giant.
ISBN 0-689-31486-8
[1. Fantasy.] I. Title.
PZ7.Z45Sh 1990 [Fic]—dc19
89-440 CIP AC

This novel is a work of fiction. Names, characters,
places, and incidents are either the product of the author's
imagination or are used fictitiously. Any
resemblance to actual persons living or dead, events,
or locales is entirely coincidental.

I

"WAKE, LLYNDRETH! WAKE AT ONCE!"

The voice frayed annoyingly at the edges of Llyndreth's dream. It was a delightful dream, too precious to lose by waking. She was standing proudly at the castle entrance as her brother rode home in triumph from the Goblin Wars. How bold and fine Rothwyn looked at the head of his army! Beneath his bright helm, the sun-bright emblem of all Solgant warriors, he was smiling at her, beckoning. Another moment and he would lean forward and—

Llyndreth burrowed deeper into layers of goose down, but the voice pursued her. "My lady, you must wake up." Rothwyn's face vanished, along with the banners and prancing steeds, leaving only a vague relief that her brother at last was home. Then a hand gripped her shoulder hard and shook that notion from her, too.

Llyndreth sat up, staring owlishly around her bedchamber. It was not morning. Nowhere near. Flickering torchlight was playing an eerie game of tag, chasing dark shadows from every corner of the room. It was her childhood nurse, Helgydd, who had roused her. In the shifting half-light old Helgydd's face looked even more wrinkled and anxious than usual.

"Helgydd," Llyndreth began to grump, regretting the dream, "it's the middle of the night. Whatever—"

Helgydd did not let her finish. "Dearest heart," she broke in, "you must flee. The underlords have risen against your brother. They are riding here now to take the castle. You must dress quickly and be gone at once. Ulm is saddling Etheryll now. The pony will be ready when you are."

Llyndreth knuckled the sleep from her eyes, hoping that this, too, was a dream. "But why?" she demanded. "Rothwyn has been a good overlord. Our father taught him to be kind and fair. Even now he is risking his life to rid the mountains of their enemies. Why should they rise against him?"

The old woman shrugged. "Once Rothwyn defeats the goblins, the Solgant lords will grow wealthy. If they dispose of Rothwyn, too, they will be all powerful. But just now, the why is not important—raise your arms, sweetness—it's haste counts for all." Stripping the nightdress over Llyndreth's head, she pointed to a pile of clothes on the bed. "Get you into these, and quickly."

Obediently, Llyndreth shrugged into a short, coarse tunic and began pulling on thick woolen hose. She was reaching for her shoes beside the bed when she stopped abruptly. "How do you know all this, Helgydd?"

The old woman pointed through the doorway, and for the first time Llyndreth saw the peasant boy crouched, head down, amid the shadows. "The underlords stopped in his village to rest their horses. And, no doubt, to fortify themselves with wine." The old woman's voice crackled with contempt. "The lord Rothwyn is well loved there, and this lad was sent to bring warning."

Helgydd broke off to give her mistress a glance of disapproval. "Will you take forever lacing up those shoes?"

Llyndreth stood up. "I'm not going, Helgydd. Rothwyn left me in charge of the castle. It's up to me to defend it."

"Defend it?" The old woman snorted. "With a handful of old servants for warriors? Armed with brooms and pitchforks? The lord Rothwyn himself could not stand fast in such case. If you stay, you will only be captured. And what then, my sunbeam? The underlords will have you for bait. Would you serve as a lure to trap your brother?"

Llyndreth sank to the bed again. How could Helgydd expect her to make such large decisions in the middle of the night without even a chance to wash her face? It was really a good deal to expect. She could scarcely believe even yet that Rothwyn's return had been the dream, while this nightmare revolt was grim reality.

"Which lords?" she asked suddenly. "Which lords are in revolt?"

"We don't know. Except for your brother, all lords look the same to the villagers. They're but grand suits of armor on horseback."

For the first time, Llyndreth began to feel afraid. "But if I don't know who's friendly, I won't know where to go."

Helgydd's gnarled fingers drew a mantle around her mis-

3

tress's neck. "You must hide, then, and put your trust in no one." Her lips brushed the fresh, young cheek. "Go quickly, my sunbeam."

Llyndreth stopped at the door. "But what of you, Helgydd?" she cried. "And of Ulm and the others?"

"They'll not harm us. We're of no importance."

It rushed over Llyndreth that she might never see Helgydd again. Suddenly the old woman who had spanked and scolded and coddled her since babyhood seemed the source of all warmth and comfort in the world. It was even harder to part with her than with Rothwyn, and she had cried for weeks in secret when her brother went to war.

Hurling herself back into the room, she made for Helgydd's arms, but the old woman shoved her away. "Will you go," she cried, almost stamping with impatience, "or will you wait to be caught like a coney in a snare?"

Uncurling himself from the shadows, the village lad took down a rush torch and lighted Llyndreth's way down the dark and drafty stairs.

Llyndreth lay on the hillside as the first gray dawning revealed the castle below. Cautiously, she parted the bushes for a better view of the courtyard. Though she could make out no faces from this distance, she could see all too well what was happening.

She had counted a half-dozen horsemen riding shadowlike across the drawbridge, perhaps a score of archers and spearmen marching behind. They had approached quite boldly, with no effort at caution. Too sure of themselves to be careful! Llyndreth thought indignantly. How different things would be if Rothwyn had stayed home!

One broad-shouldered nobleman rode a restless black stallion back and forth across the grounds, scattering chickens and pigs and ducks before him. The others held their impatient mounts in check. Meanwhile, the foot soldiers searched the manor from the castle tower to the ramshackle shed behind the stables; dragging its people out, they herded them, one by one, into a line.

He of the black stallion dismounted and stood before the prisoners. At his signal, two spearmen hauled Ulm and his stable boy, Thryn, forward. Ulm stood tall and straight, as befitted the lord Rothwyn's Master of the Hunt. Whatever he said must have angered his questioner, for the nobleman struck him with his whip.

Llyndreth only had time for a gasp of resentment before Thryn, limp with fear, pointed to Helgydd. The old woman stumbled, spilling in a heap almost on top of the lord's boots.

Llyndreth scrambled to her feet. At once the village lad, who had stood holding Etheryll steady within the cover of some trees, rushed toward her.

"Down, my lady," he cried. "It grows light, and they may see you."

"I don't care! I'll not let them harm Helgydd."

"My lady, you can do nothing." Half sobbing, he tugged at her sleeve, trying to pull her down.

He was right. Clenching her fists in helpless fury, Llyndreth sank to the ground. "If I were but a man," she told herself bitterly, "if I were a warlord like Rothwyn," how that coward would pay!" She was sobbing herself as the nobleman slashed at Helgydd with his whip, then turned away to give other orders.

She was puzzled at first. Men were scattering in every direction. What could they be hunting now? Then, as daylight tipped the castle towers golden, flames began licking at the thatched roof of the stable shed. Slowly, the rose-streaked sky darkened with smoke as the castle itself caught fire.

Llyndreth cried no longer. She lay stiff and dry-eyed watching the blaze spread; then, fighting back a hollow ache in her throat, she turned away. No need to keep the lad waiting further. No need, any longer, to dread leaving home.

She was careful, creeping back to the trees, though the lords seemed intent on their destruction below. "Let us be gone," she said in a strange, harsh voice that sounded nothing like her own. "I have a long journey ahead."

They had come to a spot where the road forked in three directions. "Which way, my lady?" asked the boy.

Llyndreth hesitated. It had been in her heart to visit Rothwyn's friend Earthrydd. Surely he and his sister, Marnne, would be true no matter what! But this morning's work had stripped her of trust in everyone.

She found her eyes straying to the path that led toward the forest and to the great, gloomy mountains beyond. It was along this road that Rothwyn had marched to war.

He had left her in charge of the manor when he rode that way. And now there was no manor. It was a hollow shell, its people imprisoned or slain or scattered. Clearly, Rothwyn should know. . . .

Llyndreth turned in the saddle. "I go this way," she said, pointing to the path.

The boy gaped at her, his eyes wide with horror and disbelief. Slowly, he shook his head. "Na, my lady Llyndreth," he said. "I was told to stay by you and keep watch. Let you just go any civilized place, I'll not leave your side. But na. I'll not go near those woods. They say there be giants there—and maybe goblins too."

"People say many things. Half the time they aren't true at all. There are goblins, of course, living far down in the mountains. But giants? I'd sooner believe in flying sheep and talking stones!"

She tossed her head. "In any case, I have to travel this road if I'm to find my brother. If there really are giants along the way—which I very much doubt—why, they can't be a great deal worse than some of our own nobles."

"My lady, please—"

Llyndreth gave him a scornful smile. "Go home, then, and say that you were afraid to follow a girl." She nudged Etheryll into action; but a few paces down the trail, she turned and glanced back. The boy stood just where she had left him, head hanging—such a downcast picture of fear and shame that she relented. After all, he had come to warn her, had followed her faithfully till now.

"Say instead," she called out, "that I sent you back. That I chose to go on alone."

Etheryll had stopped of her own accord, and Llyndreth kicked her sharply in the sides. Laying back her ears, the pony broke into a hard, resentful trot.

Let there be no more stopping, Llyndreth thought. And no more looking back. If she looked back once more— "My lady Llyndreth ..." She could hear the boy calling faintly. Llyndreth shut her ears and kept her eyes on the path ahead. On and on, it stretched toward the forest. Green and empty and friendless.

2

LLYNDRETH GAZED AROUND IN ALARM. SHE HAD LOST THE TRACK of her brother's army. It had led plain enough into the forest, then vanished. Now there was green, green, nothing but green. The way she followed, all overgrown with grass, would scarcely have seemed a path at all save that trees and bushes, draped with rank, tangling vines, grew thickly on either side. Even looking back, she could see nothing but green; she was wholly boxed in by forest.

She wrinkled her nose. This place even smelled green. The fragrance of growing things hung heavy in the still air.

"Take heart, Etheryll," she promised the pony. "We'll find our way soon. The forest cannot shut us in forever."

Or could it? There had been no crossroad where Roth-wyn's host turned off. She could not have missed it. It was as though men and horses and, yes, even the Solgant carts had all sprouted wings.

This, also, was odd and frightening: The thicket never

seemed to intrude on the path. She had not noticed at first—she had been too busy searching for the print of heavy boots and heavier shod hooves. But this last hour, Llyndreth had found herself watching for stray stalks or wandering tendrils as well. She had not found even one. Briars, brambles, tangled ropes of vine, however wild they grew outside the trail, all halted abruptly once they had walled it in.

Even worse, the narrow path seemed to be shrinking. Little by little, the living walls had closed around her until there was barely room to turn around.

It was too quiet, she discovered. Much too quiet. Muffled though they were by the thick grass, Etheryll's hoofbeats seemed alarmingly loud. Llyndreth drew rein, waiting for the complaint of a bird, for the quarrelsome chatter of a squirrel, for any sound to bring things back to normal.

Beyond her own breathing and Etheryll's, she heard only the noisy drumbeat of her heart.

Where were the birds and animals that should be nesting in the thicket? Were they—like the vines and brambles—afraid to trespass on the path?

Llyndreth licked dry lips. Her own voice, sharp with mockery, echoed through her mind. "Giants? I'd sooner believe in flying sheep and talking stones!"

Well, she'd seen none of the three, had she? And yet—She could not be mistaken about the path. It had shrunk and was shrinking still. . . .

The close quarters were making Etheryll uneasy, too. She stamped nervously and whickered for reassurance. Llyndreth patted the pony's neck. "All's well, my brave girl," she said in none too firm a voice.

She would not, she found it necessary to remind herself, have turned back in any case. The path ahead, controlled by whatever forces, might somehow lead toward her brother. Behind lay only ruins and danger.

Then, quite suddenly, it was too late to worry about giants or mysterious, unpredictable paths. Off somewhere to the right, there was a thunderous pounding, the crash of branches snapping; whole bushes, from the sound of it, were being splintered and trampled. The noise—all the more fearsome for being hidden in the tangle of brush—drove toward them, growing louder at a frightening rate. Llyndreth's throat was dry, her palms damp. She drove her heels sharply into Etheryll's side; but ahead, the path was shrinking again, and the pony could only dance about in confusion.

Abruptly, a huge white stag plunged toward them, swerved just enough to miss the pony and rider, then vanished headlong into the brush.

Etheryll was frantic with fear. There was no holding her back. But, Llyndreth saw with sheer horror, the path ahead had now entirely closed. Etheryll was bolting for the only opening left her, following the new trail broken by the stag.

Llyndreth clung blindly to her pony's reins. Her first thought was to stay seated; her second, to calm the frightened animal. But it came to her dimly, as Etheryll at last slowed a little, that the pony was galloping over smooth ground. She had stumbled over nothing; no shattered limb had reached out to snatch at horse and rider. This was no rough, fresh-broken trail, surely. It seemed, rather, as if the path itself had swerved, shifting direction as simply and easily as the stag before it.

When Etheryll halted finally, foam-streaked and quivering, Llyndreth stroked her neck and murmured soothing nonsense. It was not until the pony had stopped trembling that her mistress pulled herself erect and took stock of where their flight had brought them.

Her eyes widened at the sight before her. They had come to the margin of the forest. The wide park ahead was overspread with the same lush grass that had covered the path; here, however, it grew saddle high. Trees dotted the park—huge trees that dwarfed the high grass—and through these trees the late afternoon sun showered down in cheerful golden patches.

Cautiously, Llyndreth urged her pony forward. The white stag had vanished entirely. She could see no sign of life save the grass and trees. A gentle breeze had swept away the dead, heavy air of the path and now brushed, cool and inviting, against Llyndreth's face.

The pony came to a stand beneath one of the trees, and it was only then that Llyndreth realized how enormous they really were. In its shade she, and the pony too, shrank to the size of children's playthings.

Again she remembered the boy's warning. "Na, lady. I'll not go near those woods. They say there be giants there. . . ."

If there were giants anywhere in the world, they must

surely call this park home. Yet, oddly, she was no longer afraid. She was too tired, perhaps, for fear. Their flight along the mysterious path had drained her to exhaustion.

Stiff in every limb, she dismounted. "A moment now," she told her pony, "and you can have your dinner. Was it for this fine grass you ran so hard, Lady Mischief?" Etheryll too was at ease. Already she was trying to graze, but she nudged her mistress affectionately as Llyndreth stripped off saddle and bridle.

Llyndreth propped the saddle for a pillow at the base of a tree trunk and shut her eyes. The breeze chanted through the high grass, whispering friendly secrets that she could not quite make out. But it was not merely the breeze that comforted her, Llyndreth decided with her last drowsy thoughts. Despite the strangeness of the park, despite the odd way in which she had come there against her will, there was a peace about the place, as if there had been no quarrel here for a thousand years past. Thinking that, she drifted off to sleep.

She awoke to sunlight and confusion. It was brighter than usual in her bedchamber. She would call Helgydd to close the shutters. . . .

Her lips were forming the name when she remembered that Helgydd was far away; that she herself, who no longer had a bedchamber nor even a blanket, had slept in the open. She had never before spent a night on the bare ground, and her whole body seemed crumpled into an enormous wrinkle. She shifted onto her side. The move eased the cramp in her back and shoulders but did nothing for the ache of loneliness that swelled inside her throat and behind her eyelids until she could not hold back the tears.

Yesterday she had been so sure that she could find her brother. But today . . .

Presently, Llyndreth was done weeping. She made no move to rise but lay quite still, counting up all the things she must do. The growls of her empty stomach cried out that she must first find food. Next she would catch up Etheryll.

Then, somehow, she must rediscover the path she had lost. Or rather, the path that had, quite deliberately, lost her. The thought made Llyndreth press her cheek tighter against the warm saddle leather. She plucked a few strands of the long grass and twisted them between her fingers. How was she to find a path that could simply disappear?

Reaching for another strand of grass, her hand brushed across an exposed tree root. An odd root, she thought. Not the rough, ridged bark to which she was accustomed, but smooth—smooth as Etheryll's saddle leather.

She twisted her head for a better look, and her heart leaped, pounding, into her throat. It was no great tree root that her fingers had touched but soft, weather-stained, brown leather—leather that formed the toe of a massive boot. Her eyes traveled upward to the thongs that laced the boot together, to worn breeches, green as the leaves overhead.

"So, Solgant," a voice boomed above her. "When your race slept last in my domain, the oldest tree here had not yet taken root. No, nor its parent before it.

"And now that you've come, what am I to do with you?"

3

"WHO WOULD HAVE THOUGHT," THE VOICE WENT ON, "THAT THE next Solgant to return would be a girl!"

Llyndreth remembered suddenly how it had been when she was very small. Playing beside her father's bench, she had seen the great booted legs of his underlords. As they had towered above her, the spurs clinking wickedly, she had felt tiny and helpless and exposed. She had run, always, to the safety of her mother's arms or Helgydd's.

She was alone now, dwarfed by the voice. There was no one she might run to.

"Who gave you leave to come on my grounds?"

Llyndreth stood up. It did not help much. She found herself staring at a large, square belt buckle. Still, being upright did make her feel a trifle taller and more confident. "I did not mean to trespass on your grounds—" she began.

Coming after the giant's voice, her own sounded shaky and feather light. "Speak up, can't you?" he demanded impatiently.

She was not going to shout. If she shouted, they would both know how afraid she was. "I was only following the path," she said, "when—"

"Of course," he interrupted again. "You were following the path when you saw my stag. But then, the path is mine, too, you see. No one may travel it without my leave. Tell me what right you had to be following my path."

He was bullying her. Llyndreth began to be angry. Because Rothwyn was gone, because she was a girl and alone, everyone was bullying her. The underlords had burned her home. This nameless giant had blocked her path. All because she was alone.

"It is difficult," she said sharply, "to talk with someone as large as you are. I have to tip my head back until my neck's in danger of snapping off. And I can't see your eyes. Talking to someone's belt buckle is like shouting up an empty tower. Besides, I don't know who you are or even what you are." She was trembling, but she went on. "All I know is that you say the path belongs to you. How do I even know that's true?"

The giant didn't answer for a long while. It was so quiet that Llyndreth could hear the leaves whispering overhead. They spoke a language she could almost understand.

"It has been so long," he said finally. "I had forgotten how much you would not know. My name is Angborn, and I am an Eodan. You know that the path belongs to me, for you have seen that it obeys me.

"I had not thought of endangering your neck. As you can see," he added with a hint of amusement, "I have seldom needed to look up to anyone, yet I can see how it might prove uncomfortable.

"It has been long, so long." His voice turned thoughtful. "I suppose I can still do it. Wait a moment."

There was a curious sound that was not quite like wind rushing through the trees and a shapeless blur of mist with whirling colors at the heart of it. Then the Eodan stood before her, scarcely taller than her brother, Rothwyn.

Llyndreth gasped and drew back. "You are an enchanter, then? You can do magic? I knew that the path changed, but I never really thought—"

The Eodan began to shake his head, then thought better of it. "Well, yes. Your people would call it magic, no doubt. Whatever the Solgants cannot understand they dispose of with the word *magic*."

The girl studied him. Now that he was a normal size, he did not seem so fearful. His hair was the gray brown of old tree bark. No wrinkles had cut into his earth brown face, yet she somehow thought him old. There was neither cruelty nor kindness in his eyes; they were eyes, she thought, that had neither smiled nor wept for a very long time.

"How did you do that?" she demanded suddenly.

"The shrinking?"

"Yes, and the path too. You made the birds and animals and the very vines obey you. You must have great powers."

"Great powers? Oh, no. Once the Eodans had great powers. I never learned but a little. Much of that, even, I've forgotten."

"Yet you had me trapped," Llyndreth insisted. "Is it a small thing to have a living path at your command?"

"A small thing indeed when my people could once command rocks and rivers and the four winds. They were shape changers as well.

"And I—" he ended bitterly—"I can make myself small."

"Well, all the same, you seem powerful to me. But if you've forgotten something you really want to know, you must just find someone who remembers. I don't know how many times Helgydd had to show me the stitches before I did a respectable tapestry.

"I'm not very good at tapestry," she admitted. "When I get home, she'll probably have to show me again."

He was looking at her with an odd little half smile. "How simple you make it sound! Just find someone who has the trick of commanding mountains. But you see, there's no one left.

"I'm the last of my kind," he said. "They're gone, the others. I'm the last Eodan."

Llyndreth remembered how she had felt when her father died. If Rothwyn were gone forever too . . . and Helgydd . . . if she were to feel as alone always as she had yesterday on the empty path . . .

"How dreadful!" she said. "I'm sorry."

"You needn't be," said the Eodan quickly. "They've been gone now for many and many Solgant lifetimes. I'm quite used to it.

"Besides, I have my animals for companions. The Old Spinner in particular." Slipping a hand into the lining of his cloak, he brought forth an exceedingly hairy and hideous spider. Huge, too. If Angborn was a giant compared to ordinary men, his spinner was thrice giant. It dwarfed the largest specimen Llyndreth had ever found dangling from the stable rafters or lurking in some unused chamber of the castle.

The girl shrank back.

Angborn raised his eyebrows. "Afraid? Of a mere spider? No need. She has no venom in her—not, at least, for those I call my friends."

"Please, please, put it—put her—away!"

Angborn stroked the spider and then returned her, quite gently, to his cloak. "You are a fool, Sun's Daughter. My Spinner's a good companion and quite useful, too. Dare I hope you'll be fonder of my other friends, the trees?"

"Trees!" Llyndreth was almost sure he was making fun of her. "Trees can't walk or talk or feel. How could you ever be friends with a tree?"

The Eodan gave her a look of disgust. "What a little Solgant it is, after all! She has never heard a tree talking, so she is quite sure they cannot speak. Perhaps there is no wind either, since you have not seen it!"

"I didn't mean—"

"I will have you know," Angborn went on, "that a fullgrown tree makes an excellent conversationalist. They live long enough to know a thing or two. Much longer," he added sternly, "than a foolish Solgant."

Llyndreth flushed. It was time, she felt, to change the subject. "You haven't told me yet how you made the path obey you."

"It would be no use. You could not possibly understand."

It was insulting to be taken so lightly. "I might," she began. "You might give me a chance."

"No Solgant could understand," said the giant rudely. "They understand nothing, not even each other. Still, they do best in flocks like geese, and the problem now is to send you home to your own kind."

Home. The word made Llyndreth's eyelids sting. "I can't go home," she said. "The underlords burned it. I have to find my brother. When he knows what they have done, he will forget the goblins and come back. He will make them pay." She could not keep her underlip from trembling. "He will make the cowards pay for striking Helgydd!"

"So." The Eodan looked out across his park into the morning mists. "I had not known of this before. Sit," he said, gesturing toward the ground. "Sit down and tell me of these Solgant wars."

When she had finished, he sat silent for a long while. "Did I not tell you," he said finally, "that the Solgants know nothing? Not content with the Danturi, they must needs fight among themselves. They will master the world, perhaps, when the Eodans and the Danturi are quite forgotten. And still they will know nothing." His voice was sad but not unkind. He seemed almost to have forgotten Llyndreth.

At last he looked at her. "This changes nothing. You cannot follow your brother. If, by some wonder, you should reach his camp alive, you would find only bleaching bones."

Llyndreth sprang to her feet, her eyes flashing. "That isn't true! The goblins cannot defeat Rothwyn. He's a great warrior, a wonderful warrior!"

"He is a Solgant," said the Eodan dryly, "and therefore a fool.

"No, now. No." He disposed of her furious protests with a wave. "I'm sure your brother can handle his underlords. And handily, too. But when it comes to goblins—" The Eodan sighed. "It's the war helms that do it, most like. I've seen Solgants pass by my realm ere now. And there was never one not blinded by the grand shine of his own war helm.

"I watched your brother's band pass by. Arrogant, they were. Always, always, are the Solgants arrogant.

"The goblins will fade away like shadows at their coming. And the Solgant lords will be too busy with their war helms to look for their return."

He glanced at Llyndreth. "I've no love for the Danturi. Not I. But they have learned some patience, at least. None such as I have, naturally. But a little. It will be your brother's undoing, that patience."

"You talk of—of Danturi?"

"Goblins, to you, Sun's Daughter. Fierce, patient, cunning goblins."

Llyndreth was beginning to be frightened. He sounded so certain. "It's more important than ever, then, that I find Rothwyn. Can't you help me?"

The giant glared. "Certainly not. Solgants, Danturi, they're none of my affair, any of 'em." Watching the girl, his eyes softened a little. "Still, I did help your brother somewhat."

"How?"

"The only straight way to the mountain leads through my park. Couldn't have them trampling down my grass, could I? Hacking away at my trees?" He touched the bark of a quite old one tenderly. "They'd have shot their wretched arrows into my deer if I'd but let them.

"And so, to their good fortune, my path led them around the side of the mountain. The Danturi would be less watchful there against their climb."

"And it will have taken longer." Llyndreth sprang up, her eyes brightening with hope. "Mayhap I can catch them yet if I follow the shorter path."

"You'll take no path at all into the mountains," growled the giant. "The Danturi would catch you straightaway. All paths from my park will lead you homeward."

"Home," said Llyndreth sturdily, "is not a place. It's where those you love are." Her throat tightened. "Our lady mother died. And, next, our father. I cannot guess what has happened to Helgydd.

"Rothwyn's all I have left. If I should lose him too . . ." She looked imploringly at Angborn. "I'm not like you, my lord Eodan. I can't talk with spiders and birds and trees and —and—blades of grass.

"I love Etheryll, of course," she said, glancing at the pony, who was gazing quite contentedly. "But it's not the same.

"It isn't enough!" she added desperately. "It is not enough at all!"

She waited long and long while the trees murmured among

themselves. Perhaps the Eodan had forgotten her. Perhaps he was eavesdropping on his friends the trees.

He rose slowly. "I was remembering—" he began and did not finish.

"You are right," he said. "For a Solgant it would not be nearly enough. Fool that I am, I will take you onto the mountain. Fortune grant you do not learn to rue the day."

4

ALL DAY THEY HAD BEEN CLIMBING. ALL DAY THEIR PATH HAD
grown bleaker, more foreboding save for the occasional flar-
ing beauty of a mountain bush whose name Llyndreth did
not know.

It was still broad daylight in the open, but lengthening
shadows were beginning to cloak the sheltered areas. Llyndreth's eyes wandered often and often to those shadows.
Could she have faced them, she wondered, had she been
alone?

Abruptly, Etheryll shied and stopped, nearly throwing
Llyndreth from her back. For hours the pony had trudged
upward obediently, stumbling sometimes but never failing to
try. Now she put back her ears, rolled her eyes wildly, and
absolutely refused to budge.

"Angborn," Llyndreth called, when coaxing the pony and
kicking her sharply in the sides had produced equally disap-
pointing results. "What can be the matter with Etheryll? She
simply will not move!"

The Eodan, who had strode on ahead to make sure the trail was clear, retraced his steps. Cautiously, he looked about. "Perhaps she senses danger.

"Though if she does," he added, "this is hardly the place to stand against it. Stay with the pony while I nose about a bit."

There was a sheer drop-off on one side of the trail, a steep cliff on the other. But up ahead, cloaked in thornbushes and deep-shrouded in shadow, a ravine cut them off from the cliff.

It was into this ravine that Angborn presently disappeared. He was gone long and long. Etheryll, who never ceased to snort and dance about uneasily, was no comfort.

The setting sun splattered the cliff side with blood and fire. Could it be the same sun that shone so cheerily on Solgant fields, turning them warm and comfortable of an afternoon?

The shadows laid gnarled goblin fingers across the trail. Llyndreth found herself shivering. What had possessed Rothwyn to come upon this evil mountain? What had possessed her to follow?

Her heart leaped to her throat when Angborn finally did call out. "Nothing to fear," he said reassuringly. "She had the smell of goblin, right enough. But the rascal's wounded. Small chance of his harming us now."

The girl hurried to meet the Eodan as he scrambled back onto the trail. "Take me down, Angborn. I want to see him."

"Whatever for? Nasty creatures, goblins, at best. And this one's bloody. Scarcely worth scrambling down for, much less the climb back up."

"I want to, though," retorted Llyndreth. "Because all my

life I've heard of goblins and never seen one. Just as I'd never seen a giant till I met you."

"Oh, very well." Angborn shrugged. "If you insist on sightseeing, I must find an easier way down. Mind you stay put while I'm gone."

He reappeared presently and led her to a broken, gradual slope. "Practically a stairway. A stonemason could do little better."

The first two ledges were easy enough, but beyond that— Llyndreth lowered herself cautiously, searching for a firm foothold. Clearly, she thought, the Eodan knew many wonderful secrets. But if Angborn thought this a fine stairway, the Solgant builders had yet a thing or two to teach him.

She slipped suddenly and slid downward, landing bruised and breathless on the third ledge.

"Was I wrong, then?" Angborn muttered as he helped her up. "You'll search long for the goblin worth banging yourself about like that." He lowered himself easily to the bottom and began to shape himself larger. When his arms were level with Llyndreth's perch, he scooped her off the rock. "What a bother it is being small!" he grumbled. "A nonsensical nuisance. I could've managed that distance in one stride had I been my proper size to begin with."

Llyndreth smiled. "No doubt. And brought the trail and half the hillside down with you."

"A good thing, too, if it had carried your goblin with it. Come have your look. It grows late, and we should not be on the trail past dark." He went ahead, each massive footstep shattering small rocks, till he reached a thick growth of brush.

He flattened it with one sweep of his arm and pointed to a form slumped on the floor of the ravine. "There you are," he said, grimacing, "one goblin on display. Fortunately for us, somewhat the worse for wear."

Llyndreth dropped to her knees and stared curiously at the strangest figure she had ever seen. The goblin's leather clothes were surely meant for protection rather than for warmth. His limbs and most of his face, even to a pair of rather prominent ears, were covered with short, downy light brown hair. Indeed, the simple jacket, laced loosely at each side with thongs, showed that his body was fur-covered, too. Only around the eyes and nose, where the hair lightened and grew sparse, could you see the pale, smooth skin beneath. Dark hair, longer and coarser than the rest, fell raggedly from beneath a close-fitting leather helmet.

The creature stirred slightly, with an uneasy sigh, but he did not open his eyes or move again. One leg of his breeches was blood-soaked, slit halfway up; the shaft of an arrow protruded from his knee. On the ground nearby lay a small daggerlike knife, which was likewise bloody. Clearly, the goblin had given way to pain and weakness while trying to remove the arrow.

Llyndreth had expected to share the giant's loathing. She fought the unwelcome twinge of pity that shook her now. It was one thing to mourn, as she often had, for an innocent rabbit caught in a snare, quite another to sympathize with a wounded goblin.

Memories stirred within her. The tales she had heard as a child lying on the rushes before her father's hearth fire. Old

Gryff bewailing the merciless goblin raids on innocent villages, waving his arms till eerie shadows flickered along the wall. To her, the shadows had seemed living goblins that leaped and pounced in a grotesque, terrifying dance. Even when Gryff's cracked monotone had put her to sleep, the shadow goblins had haunted her dreams. Cruel and treacherous, they pursued her along corridors, trapped her on dark stairways, till she awoke, sobbing.

And now that she had seen a real goblin . . .

Angborn had returned his own arrow to its quiver. "Well, at least," he said, "you know now what your brother's enemies look like. If we're to make any distance before sunset, we must get back on the trail."

It was no use remembering the dreams. Or even knowing that the creature was her brother's foe. She could not hate the limp form crumpled against the rocks. It looked far too helpless, too terribly alone.

"But he'll die." Wetting her lips, she stared at the dusty, bloodstained ground. "Won't he die if we leave him?"

The giant turned to her in surprise. "Die?" he echoed. "Perhaps he will, and perhaps he won't. In either case, it's no affair of ours."

"Angborn—" Llyndreth said. "We have to help him."

Angborn opened his mouth in disbelief and then shut it again. "Don't you realize," he sputtered finally, "that this fellow is the enemy? How do you suppose he was wounded?

"Or can't you recognize a Solgant arrow when you see one?" His voice rose in annoyance. "Why, if he'd had a bit more life in him today, we'd likely be in his place!"

The girl's chin tilted at a stubborn angle. "That's probably all true," she admitted. "I can't deny a word of it. Still, we can't just leave him to suffer.

"Angborn, please." She put a coaxing note into her voice that had often worked with Helgydd. "This is a good place to camp for the night. As good, at least, as we're apt to find in these frightful mountains. All I want you to do is take out that arrow and bandage his leg. Then tomorrow we'll leave behind a little food and water. See how simple it really is?"

"Yes, indeed! Very simple. All you want to do is save one of your brother's enemies so that he can rejoin the goblin troops. If he doesn't decide to attack us first, that is. The only part that isn't simple is *why* you want to."

He shook his head. "How was I to know," he inquired of the rocks and thornbushes, "that she was mad, stark mad? Down in the forest she seemed sensible enough, if you don't count planning this journey alone. Not another wild idea all the way through the foothills. And now, the other side of nowhere, she wants to rescue goblins!

"Even Etheryll," he concluded with a reproachful glance at Llyndreth, "has the good sense to fear goblins."

Llyndreth paid him no heed. "If you won't help me," she said stiffly, "then I shall have to make do myself. I don't suppose he'd mind my using his knife—not if he knew what I was about. But you'll have to give me something for a bandage. Unless—" She fingered the hem of her tunic uncertainly. "It's more than short enough already, and no one would believe that Helgydd had it spotless when I left. Still—"

"Bones of the Earth!" the giant swore under his breath,

"but you are stubborn! No need to spoil your tunic. But I shall have to change size again. My fingers are too large and clumsy just now to deal with that arrow. And before that, I'll have to bring down the pony—who, being a sensible animal, will want to bolt. And I'll have to tie her up, and build a fire, and I suppose I shall have to wake the Old Spinner too. What a dreadful deal of trouble for nothing!"

"The spider?" Llyndreth shrank back in dismay.

"My spinner, yes. And just when she was so peaceful and content."

"But why?"

"Because she's a lady of many talents. It is she, not I, who can save your goblin. Shall I bring her forth, or no?"

"Yes," Llyndreth said reluctantly, "please do."

Once outside Angborn's cloak, the spider began daintily making her way up the Eodan's arm and across his shoulder. She did not pause till she had reached the curve of his neck, where she rubbed herself affectionately against his chin and cheek.

The giant saw Llyndreth shudder. "Like velvet, she is. The softest velvet ever your mother wore. Quite gentle too. Try stroking her and find out."

Llyndreth shook her head and withdrew a step. Angborn shrugged. "So you prefer goblins, do you? Well, there's no accounting for tastes." He held his fist up for the spider, who came onto it with willing obedience.

"Now, my good girl," Angborn addressed the spider, "it is not all to be pleasure and petting this time. I have work for you. We have need of a web, or so she thinks." Setting his pet gently in a niche in the rock, he lowered his voice into a sort of croon. "Spin for life, Old Spinner. Spin healing in your web."

Then, abruptly, he turned to Llyndreth. "Misprize her as you may, she'll do her work well. See that you do likewise. I'll make a fire, and you set water on to boil."

By the time the pot was bubbling, the Old Spinner had produced an extraordinary length of web. A thing of beauty, Llyndreth thought. If Solgant weavers could pattern so, they would be wealthier than lords. Yet there was a curious moist glimmer about it as though it had been touched by dew, where most certainly no dew had fallen.

"It will draw out the poison," said Angborn testily, "and ease the pain too, as nothing man nor enchanter has devised. If a whole goblin is what you want, this is the thing for it."

He was in no good mood yet, still grumbling. "Shrink and swell," he muttered. "Swell and shrink. I have not changed size so often in the past three hundred years. It's uncomfortable changing, if you want to know. And I shall never again fit properly into my best suit of clothes."

Angborn heated the goblin's knife in the pot and prepared to remove the arrow. "You," he told Llyndreth, "can hold his arms. There's no telling what the creature may do when I begin carving."

He scowled at her as she hung back. "Come, do your part. This is, as I recall, entirely your idea."

While Llyndreth knelt in tight-lipped silence, clutching the sinewy wrists, Angborn worked to free the arrow. "Well, that's done, at least," he exclaimed finally, tossing the cruel, barbed point aside. "You can let go now."

He need not have spoken. Feeling the goblin stiffen beneath her hands, the girl had looked down into a pair of hot, angry eyes. She drew back with a startled cry.

Suddenly, the creature swerved sideways, groped desperately for something at his belt. The something not found, he sat up slowly, favoring his bad leg, and hunched forward like a trapped, defiant animal.

"It's over here. A good safe distance away, too," Angborn remarked dryly, fingering the goblin's dagger. "And that's your goblin for you," he added, turning to Llyndreth. "Bind up his wound, and straightaway he wants to knife you."

Llyndreth scarcely heard him. Now, for the first time, she was afraid of the goblin. It was less his frantic lunge for the knife that frightened her than his eyes. Large eyes, they were, too large for the lean, downy face. A cat's eyes, fierce and lovely, their dark pupils ringed with pale, luminous amber. They put Llyndreth in mind of a wild beast, made her shudder.

At length—his strength, though not his defiance, at an end—the goblin fell back against the rocky floor. He lay, still mute, his eyes pursuing Llyndreth and Angborn savagely.

Angborn, too, was watching her, Llyndreth knew. She caught an infuriating glint of amusement in his eyes.

He was waiting for her to admit her mistake. Well, if she did, what then? It made no difference, she told herself, that the creature was hostile. She had had no reason to imagine him friendly. Nor should it matter that he had frightful eyes. He was still suffering, still in need of help.

The girl forced herself, at last, to approach him once more. "Are you thirsty?" she asked. "I could bring you water."

His only answer was a steady scowl. Flinching beneath it, she turned to Angborn. "Can he understand me, do you think?"

The Eodan shrugged. "If you know the Common Speech, you might try that."

The Common Speech? It was a tongue long out of fashion among the Solgant nobles. Yet some of the country folk still spoke it. Helgydd knew it. Yes, she herself had understood it well enough, after a fashion, when Helgydd used it talking with Oldster Gryff down in the village. Llyndreth searched the back corners of her mind for lost phrases.

Abruptly, a thought struck her. What had the Common Speech to do with goblins? If Helgydd and old Gryff spoke it—

"Angborn," she demanded, "why should he know a Solgant tongue?"

Busy about the fire, Angborn would not look at her. "It is an old language. Some things are so old that they belong to no one."

She had the words now. She could question the Eodan later. "Water—" she asked awkwardly. "Do you want water?"

Surprise broke through the goblin's defiance for a moment. He had not expected the Common Speech. But his words, when they came, were as disagreeable as his behavior. "I, Zorn, am a captain among Shadow Warriors. I have asked no help of the Sun-Spawned. Let you keep your water."

A flush rose along Llyndreth's neck. "Very well," she said, turning away. "Suit yourself, then, and do without."

Angborn's chuckle did nothing to improve her temper. "You have been treated," he announced, speaking slowly in the Common Speech so he could be sure they both understood, "to another lesson in goblin manners. They are ever ungrateful and ungracious."

It was now nearly full dark, and the companions began preparing supper. Once only, Llyndreth caught the goblin glancing toward the cook pot. Meeting her eyes, he turned his gaze steadfastly into the darkness. Yet he had no way of avoiding the savory smells that drifted through camp. They must, Llyndreth imagined, have cost him torments. But still smarting from his rudeness, she was not even slightly tempted to offer him a share.

After eating, Angborn lit his pipe. Leaning back for a comfortable smoke, he had no mind to let the girl forget what small success her kindness had met with.

"Your brother," he began, sending smoke rings swirling upward like a well-trained cyclone, "will no doubt be glad to have you bring him a store of firsthand knowledge about goblins."

Llyndreth said nothing.

"Though it will be stale news that they are a surly bunch. Everyone knows that."

The girl's gray eyes danced with mischief. "If I had paid

attention to what everyone knows about giants, I would not now be enjoying your company."

Angborn went on, unabashed. "Everyone knows, too, that they're a skulking lot, forever popping out of holes and lurking behind rocks. Though that stiff-necked specimen over there, with his talk of captains and warriors, makes them sound bold enough."

Llyndreth bit her lip. He was not speaking to her, not really. He was using the Common Speech again, taunting the wounded goblin. Not that the creature deserved her sympathy. Far from it! He had shown little enough concern for her feelings. Still—

"Little wonder, then, that they prefer darkness to the good light of day. It makes a fine cover for tricks and treachery."

If only Angborn would be silent! Llyndreth knew how much she owed him. It would be ungrateful, quite ridiculous, really, to quarrel with him over a—a creature that clearly despised her kindness. Yet the goblin's leg must be hurting. He was hungry, no doubt, and thirsty, despite his pride. And quite defenseless. To heap insults atop all that— If she could think of a way to change the subject without annoying Angborn . . .

But it was already too late. His words had done their work. The goblin raised himself unsteadily on one elbow and glared at the giant.

"True enough," he said bitterly. "We do live in darkness. We hide in holes, as you have said. And skulk behind rocks also.

"But it was not always so. There was a time when the

Danturi roamed free and proud. You would not have spoken of skulking and hiding then, old man. You would have bowed to my people then, before we tasted treachery."

Angborn glared at him. "Not so, goblin. We would not have bowed to Dantur himself. Not I nor my forefathers."

" 'Goblin,' old man? Yet Dantur was a mighty prince. I think you would have kissed the ground before him."

Angborn assumed his full size, looming over the other. "Have a care, goblin, that you do not provoke me further. I have no cause to love your kind."

The Danturin did not shrink. "Sa," he said. "I know you now, Old Man of the Forest. Her people"—he gave Llyndreth a glance of contempt—"her people mutter charms against you, calling you 'giant' and telling foolish, wicked tales." He laughed harshly. "You would not have bowed to Dantur, say you. And yet you shrink yourself to suit her Solgant pleasure."

The Eodan's huge hand knotted itself into a fist; his face, no longer kindly, was dark with anger. "One insult more," he roared, "and neither the girl's foolishness nor your wound will protect you!"

"As you will, then, if you are shamed by the plain truth." The Danturin struggled to his feet. "I will give you no cause to say that Zorn hid behind a daughter of the Sun-Born or played the coward because he was a little lame."

But even in making the boast, he swayed dizzily, and the injured leg threatened to buckle beneath him.

"Angborn!" Llyndreth cried. "Let be. He can scarcely stand!"

The giant turned away in disgust. He kicked a stick into the dying embers of their fire. "Not for pity will I let him be," he muttered. "But because he is entirely beneath my notice."

Zorn stood for a moment, his eyes fixed bitterly on the broad back; then, spent beyond endurance, he sank back to the ground.

Llyndreth awoke, shivering, in the chill, gray dawn. She pulled her mantle around her more snugly and shut her eyes. She was not ready for day to begin, not ready to face either of her companions. The Eodan was sure to be in no pleasant humor. And the goblin—her palms turned sweaty at the mere memory of the hate in his eyes.

She drowsed and woke again, with the curious sense that something—whether sound or movement, she did not know—had roused her. But all was quiet in the camp beyond the twitter of small birds and the familiar rhythmic blasts of the Eodan's snoring.

She had been dreaming of the goblin. Or what was it he preferred to call himself—Danturin? Shadow Warrior? And what lingered to trouble her was not so much his savagery, but the way he had fought to master his pain and hunger. The bitter, hopeless defense of his people. Could any Solgant soldier have done better? If one had acted so, would not Rothwyn swell with pride, boasting loudly of his army's "honor"?

And honor was the last thing she had been led to expect of a goblin.

Llyndreth squirmed on the hard ground. If she could find a more comfortable position, she might sleep again. In broad daylight these foolish, unwelcome notions might be forgotten. A goblin would once again seem a goblin and not a warrior worthy of tribute.

Long ago, he'd said, his people had roamed free. And he had spoken of treachery. Moreover, his words had some truth about them, surely. For Angborn, despite his fury, had understood well enough.

It was useless to lie here tossing and turning. She was stiff and uncomfortable and chilled to the bone. And homesick.

But the only home she had ever known lay in ashes, ruined by her own people. There was no turning back from these strange mountains where giants could be gentle and goblins honorable.

Truth, which had always seemed straight and simple before, had snarled into a confusing tangle with the wounded goblin at its heart. Without him, she could not hope to unravel her thoughts. He seemed very important, suddenly. She was anxious to know how he had borne the night.

Rising to check on him, she gave a gasp of dismay. The blanket they had given him lay crumpled in its place, stained with dark patches where his wound had bled afresh. But the goblin was nowhere in sight.

5

ZORN STARED AT THE EMBANKMENT THAT WAS HIS ONLY LADDER to the path above. He smiled briefly in bitter amusement. Brother to the Mountain Goat, his friend Gryth had often called him. And look at him now! Trapped in a miserable ditchlike ravine, pausing at a climb no more than two or three times his own height. What a rich joke that would make in the warrior camps!

Still, pause he must. He lowered himself carefully to the ground, leaned back against the very rock wall that blocked his way, and tried to find a position that would ease his leg even slightly.

He pressed a hand to his aching head, trying to sort out his thoughts. With that cursed knee so stiff and swollen, it was misery to walk on level ground, would be pure torment to climb.

And there was the thirst. How he had longed last night for the drink that Solgant girl had offered no one but him would ever know. And today was worse. He was parched already, though he had refreshed himself at a small stream after leaving the intruders' camp.

If you could call it a stream. A pitiful leak in the rocks only, no more a stream than the shelf at his back could rightly be called a cliff. Yet it had come to his aid, saved his life, perhaps, by giving him drink.

It had been all he could do to leave that trickle. And the thought of it still haunted him. It brought to mind a certain bubbling stream—one well worthy of the name—hidden in the heart of the mountains. If he were but there now, he could drink his fill of sweet, pure water and bathe his hot leg in its icy current—

He raised his head and shook it irritably. What use were daydreams? His troubles were all too real. And what right had he to dream, who might have spared himself much misery? Had there not been food and water in the outworlders' camp? There for the taking, it was, and what but his own reckless pride had turned him away?

Something inside him had rebelled against stealing that which had been freely offered. Still, he should have taken what he was sure to need. The mistake was costing him now, would cost more dearly when the sun reached its full height.

And who but a fool would hesitate to forage from his sworn enemies? Indeed, he would have done no more than his duty if he had destroyed all the travelers' provisions. They were, after all, invaders on the mountain, their very presence a threat to the Danturi. And without food or water, they must surely have turned back. . . .

Zorn fumbled at the dirty binding about his knee. Though he had tried to favor the leg, his flight had done it no good. Twice already he had loosened the bandage; but still the knee swelled, throbbed, even at rest, in knifelike thrusts.

With an effort, he found the thread of his thoughts. Say he had taken the Eodan's store of food; say the pair had gone on, foolishly, and starved on the rocky wastes. What then, but a service to his own people? Perhaps, if he had had the strength, he should even have killed the pair. But it was hard—too hard, between the pain and the thirst—to decide where duty should have led him.

Because there was the girl! There was the flaw in the stone. For, odd as it was, he had no doubt that she had meant kindly toward him. And, almost, he could have endured kindness at her hands.

He had thought she was mocking him at first. Why else should a Solgant woman offer him water? It was only when he had turned his scorn on her that he had seen the truth. The hurt shining plain in her eyes did not lie. That it had quickly changed to a glint of anger did not matter. He had seen what he had seen, and it could not soon be forgotten.

But puzzling over the girl was a luxury he could ill afford. Nor could he rest against the wall much longer. Idleness meant delay—and temptation, too. It would be so easy to shut his eyes, letting his mind drift away from his aching body.

He must instead gather his strength to reach the path above him. Everything hinged on that. Once there, Zorn promised himself, he would find the way smooth and easy.

But getting there! Less than no use, his right leg would be a hindrance. He would have to brace himself with the sound one and pull himself up with what handholds he could find.

Well, better to get on with it, then. He got painfully to his feet and, shading his eyes with his hand, studied the sunlit slope. He could see two good ledges. And yes, even before that, there to the right grew a sturdy thornbush that might, with luck, support his weight.

The thing was to put his left foot in that little chink there and then reach—lifting with his body, using his whole strength—reach for the bush. But it was a weary business when the rocks, and the bush with them, danced mockingly before him.

His thoughts whirled, too. He could manage them no better than the wavering slope. He wondered about the foreigners—were they pursuing him? Perhaps they had even passed him—though he had lost all proper sense of time and distance, he knew he had been wretchedly slow.

No, they could not have passed him. Nor did it concern him if they had.

He cared only to grasp the thornbush. Then to find another foothold. And above all, to make sure that the ledge held steady where it ought to be.

Now he had it. If he could but pull himself up, he would rest a moment, then go on—

Whether his grip failed him or his giddy brain misjudged the distance, Zorn could never afterward decide. But one moment he had grasped the ledge; the next, he was searching desperately for a foothold he could not find. He was tumbling downward, a miniature landslide crashing with him. Then his injured knee exploded against the hardest rock in the world.

Bright, searing pain slashed through him, and he slid into darkness. He never heard the startled cry from below.

ANGBORN'S VOICE WAS ANGRY. "TRULY," HE SAID AS LLYNDRETH
knelt by the Danturin's limp form, "this passes all understanding. To help the creature once was witless enough. But
then you had at least the excuse of ignorance. A child that
has burned his fingers will surely dread the fire. But you—"
He rolled his eyes skyward.

The girl stood up but made no answer.

"A baby," the giant went on, "a mere infant would have
learned by now that this goblin is unworthy of your concern.
Likely he was making straight for his comrades to bring them
down on our heads."

Stubbornly silent, Llyndreth stared at the ground. With the
toe of her boot, she traced and retraced little circles in the
dust.

Angborn spaced his words carefully as if he were speaking
to a very young and rather dull child. "Tell me then. Give
me but one reason why you should care what becomes of
him."

She looked up at last, her eyes full of trouble. "Angborn, I cannot. How can I explain what makes little sense even to me? I know he's my brother's enemy. I know he hates me and all my people. But I also know I can't leave him to die alone.

"Don't ask me for reasons, Angborn. Please. I suppose you think I'm being pigheaded. But I cannot leave him like this." She fell to her knees and began to loosen the bloody wrapping from Zorn's knee.

The giant's voice was gentler. "He didn't want your help, you know. He stole away in the night, like a thief."

"Oh, Angborn. Not like a thief. He took nothing."

"Too stupid to think of it, probably."

"Not think of food or water? Angborn, he was starving."

"Don't ask me to account for goblin behavior. I don't pretend to understand the creatures."

The stubborn knot gave way to Llyndreth's fingers. Unwinding the web, she caught her breath in distress.

"Not a pretty sight, I'll admit," Angborn grunted, peering over her shoulder. "His own fault, though. He had no business walking on it, let alone trying to climb. Spoiled a perfectly good bandage, he did." The giant gave Llyndreth a reluctant, crooked grin. "Perhaps it's no great wonder, after all, that you're bent on saving him. The one of you shows about as much sense as the other."

He looked down in weary resignation. "I shall make you a bargain. If I care for that leg once more, will you promise me three things? To leave the rascal behind as soon as he can hobble. To make straight for your brother without delay. And above all, to adopt no more goblins nor even one mountain cat or wounded wolf."

"I will swear to it, Angborn. By the sun, the moon, and the four winds of heaven."

"The whole company of which," remarked Angborn dryly, "have proved changeable sometimes. A plain, straight promise will please me better if you but hold to it."

Zorn regained his senses slowly, by degrees.

At first he felt only the sharp throbbing in his leg. Then came the heat. Heat that parched his tongue and ached in back of his eyes so that he dreamed the sun—archenemy of the Danturi—had come down from the sky to destroy him. Though he hid in caves, tunneled to the very heart of the mountain, it tracked him relentlessly—

But now and then, a delicious dampness cooled his forehead and eased his leg. He had reached, he thought hazily, the mountain stream he searched for. There, he was safe. For there, in its icy depths, the fierce sun warrior lost its power and was drowned.

At last, however, he awoke fully and knew all that for nonsense. No angry sun had pursued him, but a fever dream only. And the coolness was merely the girl—herself a daughter of the sun—bathing his face and wounded knee.

It was, he found with some surprise, no less welcome for all that. He was too weak to care whether she was friend or enemy. And much too tired to worry about his duty as a Danturin warrior.

"Here," she ordered, holding a flask to his lips, "you must drink this."

Obediently, he took what she offered. And although he could not quite bring himself to voice the words, he thanked her in his heart.

Let them do as they would with him, so long as he might rest. He had no more will to fight than he had strength to run. He was grateful, even, for his weakness. It was peaceful to lie still, peaceful to watch the sparkles of firelight dancing across the girl's shadowed face. And with that thought, he drifted into untroubled sleep.

He could have slept forever if they had let him. But twice, or three times—it was hard to remember—the girl shook him awake to spoon some steaming liquid down his throat. It was annoying at first. He did not want to eat but to go on sleeping; and his stomach, too long empty, rose in angry revolt at the smell.

But the girl was stubborn. It was something to remember about the Sun-Born. Or perhaps it came from being a woman—his mother, now that he thought of it, had been much the same. The girl would not, at any rate, be denied; but propping him up, she repeatedly thrust the spoon between his teeth. In the end, of course, he did as she wished. Which was, perhaps, just as well. The broth warmed and filled his hollow stomach, leaving him well satisfied and even drowsier than before.

Again, he woke suddenly in a cold sweat and found the giant doing something to the leg that lanced it with fire from ankle to hipbone. Still half asleep, he had almost cried out, but clamping his jaws shut, he endured in silence. Am I such a poor thing, he charged himself, that I must play the baby before this walking mountain? Small wonder, then, if he should jeer at Danturin courage! Every temptation to groan died with the thought.

Nonetheless, it took the whole of his strength to stand the ordeal quietly. He missed, in his exhaustion, the look Angborn gave him afterward. It was one of grudging respect, not far from admiration.

"It is no coward, at least," the Eodan muttered to himself. "Perhaps it is almost worth saving after all."

And although he took stock that night of their dwindling supplies, he grumbled scarcely at all about the delay.

He made up for his forbearance grandly on the day he pronounced Zorn fit to travel. "Five days," he announced irritably, buckling the pack behind Etheryll's saddle. "Five days lost, and a hungry goblin mouth to feed. Like enough Rothwyn's men will die of old age before we reach them." He turned to glower at Zorn, but the Danturin was paying no heed.

Instead, he had lowered himself to the rocky ground and was pressing his cheek flat against it. He rose presently, favoring his stiffened knee. "It is worse than you think, Eodan," he said, shaking his head. "The main road is closed to you. My people are coming, more than one of them. They are a long way off yet and will not have scented us, I think. But let one of them once catch wind of you . . ." He avoided looking at the girl. "Let you take her back, Eodan. My people do not deal kindly with trespassers. It is no place for Solgants, the Mountain of the Dark King."

Llyndreth planted herself in front of him. "I must find my brother," she said. "And my brother is on the mountain. I shall not turn back." For all that she sounded quite agreeable, she was wearing her determined look. Zorn knew it well by now; she had worn it whenever she forced broth between his teeth. "Could you not help us? Is there no other way besides the main road?"

Zorn groaned inwardly. It would go hard with him if he were caught befriending these outworlders. Some might even see it as the breaking of his warrior's oath. And he would have to travel by day when the cursed sun hurt his eyes. But he owed the girl a debt. And since she was foolish enough to go on—

"I have said already," Angborn interrupted, "that I will not have the creature as a traveling companion."

Zorn stiffened. He should have been glad of the Eodan's objection, glad of the chance to withdraw honorably. Instead, he found it annoying.

"Angborn," Llyndreth began, "I know I promised—"

"Swore, rather. By such small matters as the sun and moon."

"I will not break my promise. Yet if we cannot travel by the main road—"

"So says your pet goblin. But I have seen nothing to stop us, heard nothing."

What a fool was the Old Man of the Forest! Enchanter,

old Angborn might be, yet he was showing little of wisdom now. He would go his blundering, giant-blind way and lead the girl straight to the arms of the Shadow Warriors.

"Nor will you see anything," Zorn said angrily. "But the Shadow People, who mind the rustle of a lizard across bare rock, will hear you. Let you be sure of it. And sooner still, they will catch the scent of the four-legged beast she rides."

He did not know what his fellow warriors would do with the girl if they caught her. They were not in the habit of sparing prisoners. But a girl was different. Perhaps they would enslave her. To be sure, her very ugliness—her bald face and long, ropelike strands of sun-colored hair—would keep her safe from the men. But the women would mock her for it.

Remembering her gentle touch when he was ill, he knew without further thought that he could not let her be captured.

"There is another path," he said, "harder but little used. If the beast can travel it, I will show you the way."

Angborn glared. "And if, like great fools, we should trust ourselves to a goblin's word."

"It is a debt," Zorn said coldly. "The Danturi are faithful to their debts. In that, you may put your trust. Beyond that, expect nothing."

Suddenly, the giant's face cleared. "Very well," he told the girl. "If you will have him as guide, I'll make no further noise about it."

"Do you mean it, Angborn? Truly?" Llyndreth gave a sigh of relief. "I was afraid you'd be very angry."

"Oh, no. I'm content to have him. Quite content. He'll not be with us long, however. Not on that leg."

"But I thought you said—"

"I said he could walk on it a little. Not go striding across a mountain. If he goes with us, he'd best ride your pony."

"But Etheryll—"

"Like a wise pony, Etheryll detests goblins even more than I do. But no doubt she'll do your bidding."

Llyndreth's face puckered. "I don't know," she said doubtfully.

Zorn glanced at the pony with distaste. It was a squat, shaggy, hideous thing. He wanted nothing at all to do with it. "It will be an ill day," he said haughtily, "when a Danturin must borrow another creature's legs. Let us be on our way."

Swallowing the last of his midday meal, Zorn leaned back against a rock. The Eodan—Dantur smite him—had been right. With every step he had taken, his leg pained worse. And he was tired. Never before, save when the wound fever burned through him, had he wearied so quickly.

The girl was speaking to him. "I think . . ." she said hesitantly, and it annoyed him that she should hesitate. Everything about this misbegotten, unchancy venture annoyed him. What if the worst should happen, and he should be found in the taboo company of these outworlders?

"I think I can get Etheryll to carry you. That is, if you would care to try her."

Zorn did not look past her at the Eodan. No doubt he

would be smiling. He had been smiling for hours at the thought of seeing a Shadow Warrior perched on the backside of that stupid Solgant beast.

"Na," he said. "My leg does well enough."

"Well enough!" she cried angrily. " 'Well enough' when you can scarce drag it? Go on walking, then, and it will be worse even than when we found you. All the trouble we took will be wasted."

"Let be," Angborn said. "Can you not see he is afraid of the pony?"

Zorn's head snapped up. So that was the thought behind the Eodan's triumphant smile. Of course he was not afraid. How should a warrior who had been in battle, who had killed more than one wolf with his thrusting spear, how should such a one be afraid to sit a girl-child's pet? It was only that he, like any good Danturin, preferred the feel of solid ground beneath his feet. And that the pony, being a Solgant creature, was taboo.

"If he goes on walking," remarked the Eodan, "we shall be stalled again. By tomorrow, he'll be unable to stand." He turned to Llyndreth. "Will you wait for him yet a third time, till his companions catch us?"

He has been counting on this, Zorn thought. Counting on it that I will not ride. And he will boast forever that he found a Shadow Warrior fearful. "Let us go to the creature," he said stiffly. "My mind has turned, and I would ride like a Solgant lord."

* * *

As Zorn limped toward the pony, Etheryll gave him a baleful look. Also, she laid back her ears.

"Your good leg in the stirrup will take your weight," said Llyndreth. "Can you swing the hurt one across her back?"

Zorn took a deep breath and prepared to try. What an ugly brute it was, and smelly! The stench of it filled his nostrils.

Abruptly, the pony swung her head around, baring her teeth. His eyes narrowed against the bright sun, Zorn caught the movement just in time. He lunged out of reach, coming down hard on his injured leg and muttering Danturin curses.

Fond of him, the creature was, it seemed—as fond as he was of her. He did not like the look of those teeth. No fangs like a wolf, to be sure. But large, ugly, powerful teeth, and she had her own mind about what to do with them.

Quickly, Llyndreth seized the halter. "Shame, Etheryll," she scolded, "shame to you! Do not be so warlike. It's well enough, maybe, for Rothwyn's battle steed to act so. But it does not become you, princess of ponies. Let you be good and gentle as I bade you."

"You may climb on safely now," she told Zorn. "I shall hold her head. I should have done so before, only I never thought she'd behave so badly."

It was not what he wanted to do, climbing on. But he could feel the Eodan watching him. Let you watch, Old Man of the Forest, he thought. Let you see if I am a coward.

He swung up awkwardly. It was not much better when he was settled in the saddle. He seemed leagues above the solid earth. And he could feel the brute tensed beneath him, spine rigid, resentful and unyielding. Let Dantur smite all such Solgant beasts!

The girl watched him anxiously. "Let me lead her now," she said. "Only till she gets used to you a little."

Zorn grunted an assent.

Thanks be that his spear brothers could not see him now! Feet dangling useless in the air, his every move at the mercy of a Solgant girl! But he was not quite a fool. He knew nothing of ponies, save that this one hated him. And his leg was in poor shape for warfare if the brute had a mind to fight him further.

Other things besides his dignity plagued him, too. He was near blind from the sun; the pony smell was all around him, choking out all other scents; and he could hear little above the monotonous clop of hooves striking stone. Dantur grant that they might meet no trouble! It would be on them before he knew it.

Never before had a Shadow Warrior felt so helpless.

7

THE AIR WAS THICK AND HEAVY; ZORN'S FUR ALREADY UNPLEAS-
antly moist, though not a drop of rain had fallen. Far off, he
heard an angry rumbling.

"The storm gods grumble," he muttered uneasily. They
had been glowering already at day's end. They had sent ugly
black clouds to hurry night along, murky fingers that reached
from a gray green sky to snatch at the mountain top.

"What said you?" The girl leaned forward in her saddle,
but Zorn pretended not to hear. She called to him yet again.
"Should you not ride?" she asked anxiously. "Have you not
been walking overlong?"

He did not want to ride. The same damp, sticky air that
was causing his knee to ache had made the pony stink
more powerfully than usual. And he was more apt, anyway,
to find on foot the thing that he was seeking. They were
in need of a place to halt, a place of hiding from the storm
gods.

He mumbled something to pass for an answer and limped

on, searching for a cave, for a sizable niche in the rocks, for anything that might give them shelter.

"There is a storm coming, surely." The girl was bent on conversation. "I love storms! Old Helgydd hides in the very midst of the castle with a down pillow covering her head, but I glory to watch."

So she gloried in storms. Not he. He would be glad enough to sit snug in the warrior's hall this night, with no outworlders to plague him, swapping stories with Gryth and the rest.

To the north loomed other mountains. There already the Gods were hurling down their shafts of fire. Soon, Zorn knew, the winds would come, sweeping untethered across the wasteland between, lashing at them on the open cliffside.

The first few large drops pelted Zorn in the face. The girl would have more to glory in here on the mountain, he thought grimly, than safe inside her Solgant castle. A vast deal more to glory in.

He did not know how long they had stumbled onward, fighting the wind and rain for every step. The pony's head drooped; she picked her way carefully over rocks gone sleek and treacherous. Twice now she had missed her footing. Zorn's own leg ached abominably.

Ahead, a fiery spear struck rock; an angry god shouted triumph. Not far ahead. The smell of flame was in Zorn's nostrils. He could feel the rocks trembling beneath his feet.

Was the girl glorying now? he wondered. He stole a quick glance backward. The wind had blown her hood off once more—she could not keep it secure no matter how hard she tried—and her sun-colored braids hung sodden and heavy. Her hands were tight clenched around the reins; her face, even paler than usual. But her eyes were wide with wonder.

By Dantur's bones, he almost believed she did delight in this!

On and on he plodded. Lame. Dripping.

It was only when he did see, finally, a welcome opening in the rock that he let himself admit how tired he was. How ready to be warm again and dry.

And then, as usual, the pony must needs be obstinate. She required much coaxing while they stood shivering, all of them, in the driving rain.

"Let you get the beast inside," Zorn said impatiently. How dare she balk when he had at last found shelter! If he had the choice of it, she would learn soon enough who was master.

At last, however, they were inside the cave, Llyndreth and the Eodan wringing water out of their sodden cloaks while Zorn shook the water from his fur. They could do with a fire, Zorn thought, if only there were anything dry to use for fuel. But few things grew at this great height, and, of those, most would be soaked through beyond kindling.

He was thinking of that when Llyndreth's voice turned him abruptly. "Zorn," she said in a small, tight, fearful voice, "look you."

One glance at the cave's opening and a great sickness rushed through him. Never once since he became a warrior, nor before, when he was but a boy, had he entered a cave without pronouncing a binding spell. Who could tell what creatures, spirits even, lurked there? It was but good sense to hold them powerless.

And now, when the need was greatest, because they had lacked shelter so desperately—or perhaps because he had traveled overlong in taboo company—he had forgotten.

There in the doorway to the cave stood an icaranth, a great cave lizard as long as his arm. He would pay now—and perhaps not he alone—for his carelessness. It was too late by far for any binding spell. There was now his knife only.

"Let you hold still," he said to Llyndreth. Slowly, making as little movement as possible, he drew the knife from his belt. As he did so, he saw that the reptile's jaws gaped wide; two legs and a thin tail protruded from them, kicking frantically. Nothing more could be seen of the prey, but the lizard's body wove sinuously from the struggles within.

Zorn drew a cautious breath of relief. That the lizard had just fed might prove its undoing—and his own narrow margin of safety. If he could grasp the creature by its neck while it was still occupied with its unwilling meal and plunge his knife into its vulnerable underbelly— He poised himself to strike.

And then, beyond the pelting of the rain, he caught the sound of claws shuffling through gravel and knew that he was too late. Too late for everything this night. Too late for the binding spell and for catching the great icaranth helpless. Its mate stood beside it, and its mate's jaws were empty.

The pair stood motionless, twin lizards carved in stone, their purple-mottled bodies shining wet and gemlike from the rain, their eyes cruel and terrible and unblinking. Only the poison sac pulsing blood-red beneath the throat in sign of battle showed them alive.

Zorn's mouth went dry. He had stood some little chance before. Now there was none. While he dealt with the second icaranth, the first could dispose of its prey and be ready for him. No one could fight the two alone and hope to win.

"Eodan," he muttered without turning aside, "You seem to have some power of enchantment. Have you a spell for such as this?"

Angborn's voice was as quiet as his own. "Sometimes," he said, "I can bend animals to my will. But first I must know their hearts, as if I were one with them.

"These—these things"—he said the word with loathing—"are stranger to me. I am powerless over them."

It was no more than Zorn had expected. If he had hoped for help from these outworlders, he would have proved himself a fool. Fool twice over, he thought with grim humor. He had proved it once already by forgetting the binding spell.

The icaranth made a slight spitting sound, its call to battle. He must move swiftly now or lose the tiny advantage of first attack. If he might only have Gryth to side him—

"Guard the girl, Eodan," Zorn said hoarsely. "Take her from the cave if fortune grant the chance."

It was he who had thrown away such fortune. He must

carve it anew now with his knife blade. He gripped the hilt harder and prepared to make his move.

But quite suddenly Etheryll broke free of her mistress. With a scream of rage and terror, she reared high and came down, front hooves flailing at the feasting icaranth.

In the same moment Zorn lunged for its mate, grappling for a handhold beyond reach of the wicked snout. But despite its dainty birdlike legs, an icaranth is lightning swift. The lizard scurried beyond Zorn's grasp, swerving at once to attack so the Danturin found himself on the defensive. He made an uncertain stab with his knife, missing entirely, and felt the icaranth's sharp teeth graze his wrist.

A scratch only. For real damage the lizard must clamp its jaws and bite deeply. Zorn knew that. Yet he could almost feel the poison flaming along his arm. He could not take his eyes from the creature's swollen, throbbing sac.

With a faraway, dim part of his mind, Zorn knew that behind him the sounds of battle were dying away. How had the pony fared? He dared not turn from his own foe to find out.

His icaranth faced him rigidly, its feet wide apart and its tail extended. It might have been held fast by magic for all the movement it made. Or perhaps it was working its own binding spell of sorts—waiting for him to grow unwary or to rush in wild, blind panic to the attack.

Well, it would not find him so foolish. The creature would spring soon enough. And he would try to be ready, though he had little enough doubt of the outcome. No human warrior was so swift as an icaranth, and the stiffness of his healing leg would slow him further.

Zorn bent his knees a little, ignoring the twinge it brought him, and settled his weight on the balls of his feet.

The icaranth's tail flicked slightly and was still. It was a warning, Zorn knew. The only warning he would get—more, indeed, than he had hoped for. But even as he tensed for the attack, the stones rang with the savage pounding of hooves and the icaranth was twisting to strike at an unexpected new threat, and Zorn himself, with only a heartbeat's hesitation, was closing with the angry reptile.

No time now to be wary of his exposed arms and hands. He circled an arm across the great lizard's neck and clutched beneath its lower jaw, trying with his free hand for a clean, deadly knife thrust. But the icaranth was desperate. It loosed the jaws that had been busy with the pony and thrashed its body wildly. Its strength was greater than Zorn had looked for; and it could use its claws, too, he discovered, as they writhed and rolled across the stone floor. Its tail lashed back and forth in whiplike fury, doing little damage but adding immensely to the confusion of battle.

He had caught the creature too far back, surely! Either that or his grasp was slipping. Soon its jaws would close about his forearm, and he would be gone. But then he felt his knife sink, deep and true, into the soft underbelly flesh; and slowly, moment by moment, the icaranth's struggles grew less though the tail continued to lash convulsively against the floor.

Dragging himself free, Zorn pressed face down against the cool stone. How long he lay there, he could not have told. He was panting, weak with exhaustion and relief. Dantur be praised that he had triumphed! He had seen men die before from the icaranth's poison, and he had small ambition to add to their number. He was ready enough to die a clean and noble warrior's death. But such long, slow suffering as an icaranth bequeathed one, that would be hard to face. . . .

Presently, a hand touched his shoulder. "Are you hurt?" the girl's voice demanded.

"Na," he muttered, "I'm whole." Which was true, he supposed, though he felt battered and bruised in every part of him.

She withdrew her hand quickly, and when he rolled over and looked up, her face was white and stiff. She was carefully not looking at the dead icaranths. He could not guess what was troubling her most, horror at the battle or fear for him and her pony.

The pony! Zorn made it to his feet and stumbled across the cave to Etheryll, who stood, lathered and drooping. He forgot that she was a stubborn and unlovable beast, forgot that he detested the nauseating stench of her.

"Sa, Queen of Warriors," he murmured, throwing an arm across the trembling pony's withers and burying his cheek against her neck, "what a spear friend you are in time of need! Yours was the glory. Without you, I'd have died sure. Not even Gryth could have sided me better."

Etheryll swung her head round, and he remembered suddenly that, given the chance, she had never failed to try to bite him. He stood his ground, however, and did not flinch. If she wanted a chunk of Danturin meat, she'd earned it, certainly. But there was no question of biting this time. The pony nuzzled at him quite gently, as he'd often seen her nuzzle Llyndreth.

He stroked the sweaty hide. "At peace, are we? That's well. So it should be with spear friends who have fought a battle together." The horse stench was strong in his nostrils, but it did not seem so bad, somehow, as it had before.

It was then that he saw the blood dripping from one foreleg. He dropped to his good knee to examine the wound. When he saw the open gash and the beginnings of swelling, he cursed helplessly in Danturin. The blame was his, all his. This was what came of forgetting a binding spell.

He was still cursing, without even knowing that he had spoken aloud, when the Eodan loomed over him. "She's hurt, the pony? It looks none so bad, though."

They were strangers to the mountain. You could not expect Eodans and Solgants to know about icaranths. Nor had the pony known. "It's poison," he said, stiff-voiced. "The icaranth's poison kills."

He heard Llyndreth's gasp of horror and would not look up. "Not always, perhaps," said the Eodan. "There are some things the Shadow People do not know." Angborn spoke more kindly than he was wont to do with Zorn. "You have done your part, Danturin. Let you rest now and leave the pony to me and my Old Spinner. She will have a sore leg, like enough; but she'll not die, I promise you." Pulling Zorn to his feet, the Eodan shoved him out of the way.

The Eodan was right about one thing, Zorn thought drearily as he curled up against one wall of the cave. He would be of no help with the pony. His time for helping was past, lost forever in a moment of thoughtlessness. As for the giant's saving Etheryll, that seemed unlikely; he had never heard of even one man or beast that survived the icaranth's bite. Yet when you dealt with magic, you could never tell. And this was a question of outworld magic . . .

He did not think he could sleep. The crash of pounding hooves and the pony's shriek rang in his ears, and over and over he saw the icaranth's poison sac pulsing in the darkness. Yet he had fought hard against the storm before ever he saw the cave lizards. He heard the rain beating outside and the soft voices of Angborn and Llyndreth. The sounds came from farther and farther away. After a time, he heard nothing.

He awoke in the night to the sound of his stomach rumbling, to the knowledge that he was terribly hungry. He had not eaten since—when was it? Before the storm, surely, and even then, not nearly so much as he had wanted.

But then, more fully awake, he remembered the battle and the wound on Etheryll's leg, and his hunger vanished. He tried telling himself that the pony was only a pack animal. It was not as if Gryth had been bitten, or another of his spear brothers. But it was no use. The pony had saved his life; that had wrought a battle bond between them such as he'd shared with few two-legged warriors.

He sat up slowly, needing to know yet dreading the answer. "How does the pony?"

The Eodan was blowing smoke rings, and Zorn wondered dully how he had gotten sparks to light his pipe. "She does well enough." Angborn sounded a little snappish from lack of sleep. "I told you the way of it before you slept. Could you not believe me?"

He did not believe even now. Rubbing at his eyes, Zorn came forward to see for himself. The pony stood drowsing, her eyes half shut. Her injured leg was wrapped in the shimmering stuff of Old Spinner's web. It looked swollen, to be sure, but not nearly so much as he had feared. And the icaranth victims he had known of had not drowsed; they had cried out in agony and horror, longing to die.

Never again, Zorn thought, would he scoff at Eodan magic. He felt grateful to Angborn, more grateful than he had supposed he could be; and rushing back, hand in hand with the gratitude, came his hunger. He remembered that he had slain fresh meat.

He glanced about the cave. There were stains on the rock, here and there. All other signs of the struggle had disappeared.

"The icaranth I killed, what came of it? They're good to eat if we had a fire for the roasting."

The Eodan's eyes glinted. He was not above hunger, then, whatever ancient powers he might hold. He patted the area of his cloak where the pet spider clung against his heart. "My spinner here, she's webs of many kinds. She can spin fire well enough at my asking. A fine, dry web, brittle as graveclothes, that will catch at the slightest spark."

Zorn turned at a slight, wordless sound from the dark of the cave. He had thought Llyndreth was sleeping. "You'd not eat them?" Her face was white and stiff, the same look on it he'd seen just after the battle.

"And why not? Icaranth's a delicacy, my people think." When we can get it, he added to himself. No need of saying it was seldom hunted because of the danger. That would sound like boasting, perhaps, or make Danturin courage sound small.

She did not look at all cheered by his reply. What foolish Solgant notion was working at her, Zorn wondered. Did she think herself too fine for lizard meat?

"But this cave," Llyndreth said in a small voice, "it belonged to the icaranths.

"It was their castle," she went on when he did not answer but only stared at her in puzzlement. "They only fought to save it. And now you would make dinner of them.

"I know," she finished in an even smaller voice, "what it is to see your castle fall."

She could not expect him to go hungry because of such silliness. "It is only an icaranth," Zorn said hopefully.

"So!" It was surprising how much venom she could put into a single word. "And yet I have heard men say 'only a goblin,' too."

Zorn turned on his heels and stalked from the cave. If that was what she thought of him, if she held him no higher than an icaranth— Let her go hungry, then. It was her own belly that would suffer, not his.

Drawing his knife, he knelt beside the carcass. There were good steaks here for the taking. His stomach rejoiced at the prospect.

The rain pelted the back of his neck. She would regret her stubbornness when Angborn had a good fire going. When she smelled the savory odor of roast meat, she would be sorry.

Zorn touched his blade to the lizard skin. She had fed him, spoonful by slow spoonful, when he was ill.

He grew wetter. He had squatted on his heels so long that his stiff knee was aching. His belly squalled at the delay. She would be watching him, each mouthful he took, and still she would refuse to eat. He knew in his heart that each morsel would choke him.

Reluctantly, he sheathed his knife and stood.

Zorn was drenched when he returned to the cave. He dumped onto the floor of the cave an armload of bulbous, purplish roots. "Let you roast these on the Eodan's fire, then pound them with a rock," he said ungraciously. "They'll serve for food in lack of something better."

"How is it, Danturin," asked Angborn when they had finally eaten, "that you dined meatless tonight?" There was mocking laughter in his voice. "You made sport of me once, saying I shrank and swelled to suit a Solgant's pleasure. Has the Shadow Warrior captain also fallen so low?"

Zorn did not answer. He was dry, for once, and drowsy, and his stomach had more or less quieted. There was the pony alive to be thankful for, and the look Llyndreth had given him when she scooped up the roots from the floor. There was something in that look almost better than a full belly. Almost, he had stopped regretting icaranth steaks.

8

THEY WERE SNUG ENOUGH IN THE CAVE WHILE THE PONY'S LEG was healing. Meanwhile, Zorn's own leg grew stronger so that he scarcely remembered it had been unsound. He forgot other things also. Forgot that the girl and her pony had once seemed ill-favored and foul-smelling. Forgot his misgivings about Danturin duty. Forgetting comes easy in a cave-sized world with the rain beating down outside.

On the third day it cleared, and nothing would suit Llyndreth but that she must go out to hunt for firewood and roots. Zorn went willingly. It was true that the bright sun hurt his eyes—and true also that he had already foraged by night. But the mountain air was clean and cool with a fresh-washed scent to it. Such air sang in your veins, and it was that, he supposed, which turned wood gathering from a chore into a pleasure.

They were on the point of turning back, though Llyndreth was loath to do so, when she saw the thornbush.

"Look!" she cried. "Oh, Zorn, look there!"

Squinting hard against the glare, he did as she bade him. It was a quite ordinary thornbush, actually, of the kind his people knew as Dantur's Flame. And it had bloomed in a perfectly ordinary way, as such a bush always did in gratitude for a good rain.

But it *was* beautiful, red as the heart of fire and blooming all alone against a shelf of barren rock. If you had never before seen such a bush—

Half-ashamed of the impulse, Zorn set down his burden. "If you wish a branch—"

"No. It would only die, and I could not see it anyway in the darkness of that miserable cave."

She touched his arm. "Take me up there, rather, so I can see it up close."

Zorn drew back. She had touched him before, no doubt, from time to time. When he was ill, she had surely touched him. But not like this. Not in the light, unthinking way that one might touch a friend. It reminded him sharply that she was Solgant. That such contact must surely be taboo.

Shoving the thought from his mind, he helped her climb to the thornbush. If he was breaking taboo, he was not sorry. How could he be sorry when she looked so at the flower, silent and breathless, as though he had given her a great gift?

He wanted suddenly to tell her that his mountain held many beauties she had not seen. Rushing walls of water that no Solgant creation could match. Great carvings of stone within the earth that no mortal hand had fashioned. Gemstones glittering in cave walls.

But he said nothing. She was a Solgant, after all, and perhaps she would not think such things beautiful. There was little telling about a person who would not eat icaranth!

Besides, Angborn had said the pony might travel tomorrow. They would make haste toward the Solgant camp; once there, his debt would be paid. His people—and he with them—would drive the Solgants from the mountain.

The girl would never see the things he cherished, nor would he see her again. . . .

He had tired, he found, of thornbushes and was anxious to be gone. "Must you stand there gaping till moonrise?" he asked sourly. "Have you no flowers of your own below the mountain?"

"We have them, yes." Though she was at pains to keep her voice steady, he heard the hurt in it. "But none so beautiful as this. It was the most beautiful flower I'd ever seen."

Was, she said, as though he'd spoiled it for her. Well, small wonder if he'd snapped a little. It had been pure foolery, bringing her up here. His eyes ached miserably in the midday glare. Once he was well rid of these day travelers, he would never show the sun his face again. . . .

Neither he nor Llyndreth spoke till they had reached the cave.

And that night Zorn heard whispers in the rock. The rising whisper of Shadow Warrior feet.

Panic rose in Zorn. He had not looked to find his brother warriors here. No one used this old trail anymore. It had belonged to the Old Ones, to those who had owned the mountain long ago; though the path itself was not taboo, there were places along it where no Danturin had leave to go.

Yet there were Shadow Warriors behind them! And if they were discovered—

Noiselessly, Zorn paced the ledge in front of the cave. He himself could leave the path and lose himself on the mountains. Not his companions. They were tied to the path; no binding spell could hold them tighter. And they could not outrun the Danturi—

He might leave them now. There was yet time. Even—*he might yield them up.* The temptation flared in him, then flickered out. He would have to live with himself if he did that, would have to live with the girl's eyes.

Yet if he were found with outworlders . . .

Dusk deepened to full night, then quickened with the promise of the coming moon.

It was then that Zorn remembered the tunnels. Not content with open roads, the Old Ones had carved out great corridors that ran underground to their places of power. And these the Danturi shunned twice over. Indeed, some long-forgotten member of the priest-kind—jealous or fearful of what magic might lurk there—had given an order that they be sealed off.

Long ago. And if you wait long enough, all seals are one day broken. So it was now with some of the great rock heaps that shut off these ancient corridors.

Perhaps the rains of long, slow years had done it, or perhaps the mountain itself had trembled under attack from the storm gods. However it was, first one and then another of the sealing mounds had begun to crumble away.

In his boyhood ramblings, Zorn had come, time and time again, on such half-opened tunnel doors. They had beckoned with their mystery, beckoned all the more because they were forbidden. He'd had half a mind to break taboo and enter one.

Yet the breaking of taboo was a fearful thing. You could not tell whether binding spells would count for anything in such a place. And besides the terror, there had been the sheer labor of it. Such opening as there was would not give easy entrance; the widening of it had seemed a giant's task.

Things were different this night. This night Zorn was in company with a giant.

It was a moon of hope. It had shown Zorn the thing he sought. Now if Angborn, with his great strength, could clear away the rubble, they had one last good chance of safety.

Urgently, Zorn shook the Eodan awake and told him of the new peril. "If the warriors rest through high daylight," he said, "we shall win through. If not—

"But I hardly think they'll be in such a hurry. It is painful for a Shadow Warrior to travel in sunlight"—he could say it now without dishonor, without seeming to complain—"and they will not expect outworlders to be burrowing inside the mountain."

They worked past moonset, the three of them—Eodan, Solgant, and Danturin—and past the dawn without stopping. But old Angborn would not have missed their efforts much,

Zorn thought, if he and the girl had napped the whole time through. For it was only the Eodan, shifted to his full size and grumbling constantly, who could handle the great rocks as though they were playthings.

"Now, Eldeon, my grandsire," Angborn fretted, mopping at his moist brow, "or my father, even, could have made the rocks do his bidding. Though they were mighty men, my forefathers did not strain their backs for nothing. They were mighty of mind also, the true Eodans were."

Llyndreth had her regrets also. "If only we had a little cart," she said ruefully, "we could hitch Etheryll to it. That's the Solgant way of clearing rock."

As for Zorn, he wasted no thought on might-have-beens. He wanted only to finish in whatever way they could and to see his companions safely away.

Not that he could be sure the way was safe. Who knew what powers those tunnels guarded? He cast the thought roughly from his mind.

The sun had pained him for long and long, had passed overhead and begun its descent into darkness when they were at last finished.

The Eodan stepped back and studied his job critically. "That should do it," he said. "Not but what my grandsire would have done a neater job. A fine mess the two of you have left!"

Looking into the black depths, Zorn trembled. It had been one thing to help the girl. It was quite another to go against a taboo so ancient. He had a sudden vision of old Hrald, the high priest. You could not see Hrald's face, hidden deep within its hood, but the gnarled and bony fingers pointed at him in accusation.

Nevertheless, he was first inside the tunnel. He muttered the words for safe making a strange place, the ones he'd forgotten at the icaranth's cave. He was not at all sure that they would help in a taboo place, but he would do his best. He would not fail his companions yet again.

Stepping out into the dazzling light, he found Llyndreth peering inside. "Pew!" she exclaimed with disgust. "It smells dead in there. It has the smell of moldy boot leather.

"And it's even darker than the cave. No one knows how much I hate the dark!"

There you had it, Zorn thought bleakly. Ever the Danturi loathed the sunlight. Ever the Solgants dreaded darkness.

He thought it best to be blunt. "You will be longer in darkness if my people find you. There is sunshine to be found at the far end of yon tunnel." Dantur grant, he added to himself, that it be true.

Still, she held back. "You and Angborn go first, at least. Etheryll and I will follow."

Zorn stared at her, blinking. Did she not know? Had she no brains at all? It was a time for further bluntness, but somehow he could not say the words.

He turned to the Eodan instead. "I cannot tell where the tunnel may end, but it will take you from the danger here at least. Let you be wary coming out."

"You're not going with us!" It was as though she had called him "goblin" to his face, the way she said it. Zorn tried to be angry and could not.

Surprisingly, the Eodan came to his defense. "He cannot come with us," Angborn told the girl. "Think, Llyndreth. He could not go back to his people if he led us through that tunnel. There would be no turning back.

"Is that what you would ask of him?"

"No," Llyndreth said slowly, "of course not." But she said it stiffly.

It was an ill parting, Zorn thought. As all things had been ill between them since they left the thornbush. He would set things right once more if only he knew what to say. The Danturi were not noted for fair speech.

"Fortune shield you, Danturin," old Angborn said. It was spoken in all courtesy, the kind of leave-taking one gave an honored friend, but Zorn scarcely noticed. He muttered something in reply. It was only as Llyndreth was leading the pony to the door of the cave that he thought of the one thing worth saying.

"The thornbush flower," he said. "It was a thing of beauty. I am glad in my heart that you saw it."

He strode away quickly. It was best not to look back. He would not turn, would not.

By the time he did, at last, glance back, there was nothing to be seen. Only the tunnel's opening, a black scar gouged against the face of the rock, and the scattered rubble that cried out against broken taboos.

THE THING FOR IT, ZORN DECIDED, WAS TO PUT AS MUCH DISTANCE as possible between himself and the tunnel. He could make good time now that he was no longer bound to a single, winding path. His leg felt good—strong and sound, without a hint of stiffness. He could clamber down, picking a way that would have dizzied his late companions, using the road only when it suited him.

He would head straight for his brother warriors and try to act as though the meeting were by chance. He did not know how he would fare at deception; never before had he lied to anyone. But he had always believed in going up against a thing boldly. He supposed this case was no different.

Beyond that, he could plan no further. He would have to see what fortune chanced and depend upon his wits to help him through. Dantur grant them sharpness, he thought wryly. He would not be dealing with an icaranth now.

Secure behind a rock, Zorn peered down on the Shadow Warrior encampment and smiled inwardly. For the first time in many days, fortune seemed with him. Given the mess he'd begun with, things could scarcely have fallen out better.

Some of the Danturi still slept while others were stretching lazily and yawning. That they had bedded down for the day showed that they'd been in no great hurry. That was good, very good, as was their smallness of number. But best of all, it was Guroc in command.

Of all his fellow warriors, save only Gryth, it was Guroc whom Zorn knew best. Growing up as hearth friends, they had shared much sport. Were Guroc not a scant half year younger, they would have joined the Warriors together.

With Gryth or Guroc, he should have less explaining to do. Of the two, he was rather glad to find Guroc. He would have hated lying to Gryth.

Zorn hailed the camp. Cupping his hands in the Danturin sign of peace, he sauntered up as though he'd just returned from an hour's scouting. But he was careful to show Guroc all the honor that was due to a commander.

"I give you greeting, Guroc, Captain of Shadow Warriors. May you have good hunting this night, and health be to all at your hearthstone."

If Guroc felt any joy at Zorn's arrival, he hid it valiantly. Yet Guroc had never been one to make a show of feeling.

He rose now from the rock where he'd been sitting and

regarded Zorn silently. "Sa, Zorn, sister-son to Gerd," he said finally, not bothering to give back Zorn's own title of respect. "Whence came you? Never was one more aptly named for shadows.

"When we sought you, you melted before us like mist. And now, like that same mist, you steal upon us."

Caution pricked Zorn. This was not the sort of greeting you looked for from a friend.

"How mean you, Guroc?" he asked quietly. "I have never hidden myself from my spear brothers."

"Na? Yet you were overlong away, Gerd's sister-son. King Myrgg fretted after you and Gryth also. They thought their prince of spies lay rotting in some Solgant ditch."

Zorn's stomach knotted, fistlike, inside him. He had neither said nor done anything amiss, yet already Guroc was coldly hostile. If something or someone had turned Guroc's ill will against him, he was but a wrong word or two from disaster. Perhaps the truth, or a half-truth, at least, would serve best for the moment.

"So I nearly was, Guroc. For a Solgant arrow caught me. Yet fortune was with me, and it was not my time to die—"

He was saved, for the moment, from explaining further; for something struck him a hearty whack between the shoulder blades. "Zorn!" cried a familiar voice. "Hearth brother!" Turning, Zorn found himself being alternately clasped in Gryth's arms and pounded affectionately.

Here was no lack of welcome. Shadow Warriors were not supposed to forget their dignity so far as to shout and wrestle with one another. But then Gryth would one day be king, and rank carries its privileges.

At length, when Gryth had brought his joy under control, Zorn looked at him in some puzzlement. Gryth and Guroc were equals now in rank; yet he had, from his hiding place in the rocks, watched Guroc giving orders while Gryth still slept. Only one could be commanding—

"How came you to be here, Gryth?" he asked. "With Guroc's troop, I mean."

Guroc himself answered. "Because he is the king's sister-son and would not be denied. It was not enough that Myrgg should send me and my warriors forth to find you when we were better sent against the Solgants. Na, Gryth himself must come in search of his heart's brothers since we could not be trusted—"

"There was no lack of trust in the matter," Gryth said reproachfully. "It was only that I could not think Zorn in trouble and not go. We have been all our lives like cubs dropped in the same hour."

"Do I not know it?" Guroc answered shortly.

Gryth paid no heed to the bitterness of the answer. He was busy with Zorn again. "Faugh!" he said, "but you do stink. It is enough to fell a hero. What have you been about to smell so dreadful?"

Zorn tensed. He had splashed in a stream on his way to camp, trying his best to rid himself of alien scents. But he had ridden the pony, stroked it. Both Angborn and the girl had touched him. They had slept side by side within the cave. Like enough, there were odors clinging to him yet. His own nostrils had grown so well used to the stench that he could no longer tell.

"Is it possible," asked Guroc softly, "that the king's heir has never before smelled those beasts the Solgants ride?"

The camp grew quiet. It had scarcely seemed noisy before. But now you could hear the wind wailing mournfully along the rocks and no sound else.

"It is very like," Zorn said, "that I carry Solgant smells about me. There was a party of outworlders wandering about. I tracked them for some nights. Once, indeed, I slept the day through where the stones were still warm from their bodies."

"It was so that you must have picked up their scent," Gryth agreed with relief. "It would have been strong about their sleeping place."

"Yet scent fades with time, as the least of our boy hunters know." Guroc's eyes were glittering. "The scent is strong about you now, captain of spies.

"Tell me more of these outworlders. Who were they, and what did you with them? Is it that you followed them only and let them to roam free across our mountain?"

"Sa, Guroc. I followed only. It was in my mind to learn where they might go and why."

"And?"

"They went nowhere at all, for they turned back. They were no warriors, certainly—no prey of honor that a captain might boast of. There was a Solgant girl and her beast that you say I smell of, those two and an old man. They were lost, I think, and in time they turned back."

"Think you they wandered onto the mountain with no purpose? They climbed high indeed by accident."

Zorn shrugged. "Perhaps they lost their purpose in meeting with our storm gods."

"It was the storm gods, then, that turned them back when a Danturin warrior was at hand?"

"I have told you." Zorn kept his voice even. "They were not worth the taking. Had they made any warlike move or tried to join with others, I should have killed them. Let you believe it!"

Lies. Lies woven in amid truths like golden threads amid black ones. He must be careful or those bright threads would entangle him! He was trembling inside, fearful. He had never felt so going into battle.

"So they turned back," mused Guroc. "How long since?"

One day ago? No, two. He must not place them too near the tunnel's entrance. Yet it must seem worth Guroc's time to turn back after them.

"Two days past," he said.

"Think no more of your outworlders, then." Guroc smiled for the first time. "Before this night ends, Zorn, you shall question them yourself. For we, also, have caught their trail, and it was in my mind that they might well turn back." His smile was no pleasant thing to look on.

"Do you not think it a great wonder, spear brother, that they came so far alone and, all unaided, found so little-used a path? I thought it so, at least. Surely, thought I, they will lose their way at last. Unaided, they must finally turn back.

"So I set two warriors to greet them on their return, down

below where they missed the main road and came up all this way by chance."

Zorn's heart sank. This was ill luck, the worst possible. Guroc need not turn back to learn the truth. His own falsehood had bought no time for Llyndreth but had only trapped himself.

"Well done, like a wise captain, Guroc," he managed to say through the fear that swept over him.

"Would you not have done the same yourself, Gerd's sister-son?"

Guroc sounded malicious and vastly pleased with himself. Already he was guessing at Zorn's lie. Soon, all too soon, the guessing would end.

Then Guroc and his fellows would go searching for the outworlders. They would find the scattered rubble and the unsealed tunnel. And they would know—

Zorn could not fight back the fear. Even if King Myrgg should be merciful toward him for Gryth's sake, he would have the priest-kind to deal with. He tried not to imagine what they would do to one who had broken their ancient taboo.

He must escape. He saw that with unblinking clarity and did not dare think further. How had he gotten himself into such a muddle? Why in Dantur's name had he been so ready to help the girl?

Guroc was speaking to him again and must somehow be answered. "You spoke of a Solgant arrow," he said, staring at Zorn's leg. "It would seem you wear a binding still. What thing is that you tied your leg up in?"

"Spider's web." Zorn tried not to look uneasy. He should

have stripped off the remnants of Angborn's last binding. But it was no Solgant thing, at least. Guroc could prove nothing against him, surely, from the soiled and tattered strands. Did not his own people use spider's webbing for wound healing too?

"A spider's web? Never have I seen a spider that could weave so." Guroc motioned to the king's heir. "Let you be judge, Gryth. Let you look closely at his 'spider's web' and say if any spider made it."

Gryth knelt by Zorn and, with a quick glance that asked forgiveness, unwound the bandage. He studied it for a long time, then looked questioningly at his spear brother.

"Well?" demanded Guroc.

"It is something like spider's web, surely. And yet ..." Gryth hesitated, "... yet it has a pattern to it that no spider I have met with could manage. And it is longer and sturdier than any I have seen."

"For all that," Zorn said, without much hope, "it *is* a spider's web, and I did find it on the mountain."

Gryth would not look at him. Guroc was looking, though. He grunted in satisfaction. "So also you found Solgants on the mountain. Most like you found the two together." He turned to the youngest of his warriors. "Lurth. And you, Darion. Let you bind the captain with leather thongs."

Zorn stiffened. This was some daylight fright dream, the kind from which you presently awakened dazed and sun blind. It could not be that Guroc, whom he had counted friend, would disgrace him over a mere spider's web.

But Gryth's cry of angry protest, that was real. "You cannot do so, Guroc. What need? You have no reason to bind him, no proof!"

"No proof? He reeks of Solgant. He let the outworlders pass unharmed. It came not from this mountain, the binding on his leg. What more proof do you require?" He shook his head. "Na, Gryth. Your love for a spear brother blinds you. It is well that I, not you, am in command."

He nodded curtly, signaling Lurth and Darion. It flew into Zorn's mind to make a fight of it though he would doubtless be overpowered in the end. But he had never yet struck a spear brother, and he was not ready now to do so.

Not only was it one more taboo offense—almost, he had lost track of those—but he held no anger in his heart against Lurth or Darion. They were but doing their duty and not liking it overmuch either, from the looks of them. They refused steadfastly to meet Zorn's eyes.

No fright dream, this, because it was a thing beyond dreading. Asleep or wakeful, he had never imagined himself a prisoner to his own kind. He who had treasured honor above all else. He who had stood side-by-side with the royal heir and was held like a hearth son by King Myrgg himself.

And Guroc, whom he had trusted, was rejoicing at it.

Well, what had come had come. Let him bear it with what dignity he could. Bear it for now and think afterward what chances he might have. Silently, unresisting, Zorn held out his arms.

They bound him in such fashion that he could have some use of his arms in climbing and looped another, much longer coil of leather around his waist so that he went on a leash like some Solgant dog-pet. Zorn thought once how it would be to enter Myrgg's court led so. It was a brief thinking. He would never let himself be dragged before the king. Never.

Despite the looseness of his bindings, it was hard work managing the steeper slopes. He was not used to going bound. With each movement, it seemed, he managed to strain against the leather so that it cut into his flesh with a painful, enraging jerk.

He fell once. Not a bad fall, but it knocked the breath out of him for a little and let him know that the fresh arrow scar in his knee could cry out against abuse.

Gryth was with him at once, muttering angrily under his breath.

Zorn did not fall again. Gryth saw to that. Gryth, who hovered at his shoulder as though he were some fledgling with a broken wing. Gryth, who looked ever more miserable, as though he, not Zorn, must struggle against the bonds. Gryth, who believed now and would soon believe no longer . . .

Once, in his anguish, Zorn lashed out at him. "Can you not let me be?" he cried. "I do well enough on my own."

Afterward, Gryth took pains to keep out of sight. He could have spared himself the trouble. Zorn could feel his nearness. Lacking sight or sound or smell to tell him, he would still have known. That was how it had always been between him and Gryth. . . .

The rising sun found them on the Old Ones' path, not far from the mouth of the tunnel. A hawk wheeled lazily against the rosy promise of light. The thought came to Zorn against his will: *The girl Llyndreth would find that beautiful.* Well, he found it none so ugly himself. If the sun could stay so gentle always and not rise, fearsome and glaring, to cast spears of fire against Danturin eyes—

Then the hawk soared. *Free,* Zorn thought. *Free!* And he forgot notions of beauty, Solgant or Danturin.

When Guroc at last called a halt, Zorn could not sleep despite his weariness. He pictured himself bound at King Myrgg's feet, Guroc holding the tether. It would be Guroc, he was sure. Why else had his one-time spear brother been so keen to doubt his honor? No one else would have. None but Guroc.

Perhaps Guroc was busy with the same vision, because Zorn opened his eyes of a sudden to see his captor looming over him.

"How is it," asked Guroc almost gently, "with the king's favorite?"

Zorn made no answer. Could Guroc truly expect him to whine for mercy? He might wait long and long for such a triumph.

"If you led us to the outworlders, you might not be brought before the Council."

That was both lie and mockery. Guroc's whole troop had seen him taken prisoner, had heard what their captain said of him. King Myrgg must try him now. He could not choose elsewise.

It might profit Guroc if he should betray the girl and her Eodan now; himself, it would profit nothing.

"They turned back, I told you."

"Sa. We shall see."

There was one thing more to be spoken between him and Guroc. Zorn said it now. "I held you friend."

He was careful not to make a plea of it, nor even a question; yet Guroc answered it.

"Friend!" Zorn marveled at the bitterness of the echo. "Friend," Guroc repeated. "Ever you have stood between me and the things I dreamed of. Ever you were one half-year the stronger, the swifter, the surer of foot and arm and eye.

"Can you not remember how often I came in second, when we were boys, in the throwing of spears at a mark? First but for you, Zorn, Gerd's sister-son. You were warrior before me, captain before me, eyes, ears, and nose to the king whilst I—"

He did not finish. "Then there was Gryth," he said, his voice hardening further. "I might have been first friend to the king's heir. Yet it was ever Gryth-and-Zorn, Zorn-and-Gryth, as if you were halves of one whole split in two at birth.

"We are of an age, Gryth and I. It should have been me, not you!"

Guroc did not try to hide the long hurt in his voice, and almost Zorn pitied him. Almost.

But it was not Guroc who would be dragged in disgrace before the Council.

"Sa," Guroc went on presently. "I was glad when you did not return. Glad of it in my heart. And then, because we were friends, old Myrgg must send me in search of you when I might have done battle with the Solgants. And Gryth, he must needs come too so that—even in death, as we mostly thought—you made a pair with him still. Even then I, Guroc, was let to come along.

"I thought it a bitter cup, spear brother. However," he said, smiling, "the draught is none so bitter now."

He left Zorn then, left him squinting, without hope, into the morning sun. It was his own fault, Zorn told himself dully. He had been too proud, had believed his honor beyond suspicion. But he had not guessed he faced such hatred. Had he known, had he only known—

It was not only he and Guroc who were wakeful. Past midday, probably, Gryth came to him.

"Sleep now," he told Lurth, who was standing guard. "I will watch the prisoner."

"But Guroc-Captain gave orders—"

Gryth drew himself taller. "Think you that Guroc outranks the king's heir?" He was not above going haughty when it suited his purpose. In the past it had amused Zorn sometimes. He was not laughing now.

"By Dantur, it's hot." Gryth threw himself down beside Zorn, panting. He peered anxiously at his friend. "How is it with you, Zorn? You must be all over bruises and leather galls."

Gryth did not look as though he'd slept at all, but there was an air of determination about him. "It's wrong," he said. "I've thought it all out. It's wrong for Guroc to treat you so and wrong for me to let him. I'll not let him."

He whipped his knife from the sheath and sliced neatly through Zorn's bonds, setting his hands free.

Free. Like the hawk sailing against first light. Free, as he'd always been before.

But not for long. Not after Guroc's warriors joined them. Not when they knew he had broken taboo to help an enemy—

"Guroc will be whopping mad, of course," Gryth was saying. "I'd be, too, in his place. His command and all.

"But it's for his own good as well, when you think on it. He said I was letting what I felt blind me, seeing what I wanted because you're my friend. But it's what he's doing, I think, seeing what he chooses. He wants, somehow, to believe you a traitor. And they'll laugh him out of Council when he brings the charge."

They'd not laugh, Zorn knew. He remembered the Council warriors, stern and solemn and unyielding. He remembered old Hrald, the high priest, smelling of sacred smoke, his withered body shrouded in cloak and hood. How could he face all that?

Free but for Gryth's stopping him. Yet to go free, he must betray Gryth.

"You'll be in disgrace, both of you." Gryth leaned back on rock, shutting his eyes against the glare. "Guroc will seem an ill-meaning fool. And you—well, there's some who will believe the worst always, any chance they get. Somehow I must make old Guroc think better of the business. . . ."

Reluctantly, Zorn's fingers curled around a stone. How could he will that hand to strike Gryth—good, faithful Gryth, a spear brother without fault, who was willing to defy Guroc on his behalf? Perhaps he could tell Gryth about the girl; perhaps if he could make Gryth understand . . .

But then Gryth, too, would be in trouble. Might even have to face the Council in his stead. Better that Gryth's head should ache for an afternoon. Better even that Gryth should learn to hate him . . .

Gryth talked on, his eyes shut trustingly. With any other, it would have been easy. With his hearth brother, it was very, very hard.

Zorn clutched the rock and brought it down with care. Hard enough to stun, not hard enough—Dantur let it be so!—to injure greatly.

Then he had Gryth's knife and the leather coil they had bound him with, and he was moving. Quietly, at first, to give no warning of his escape; then swiftly, with less care, to put distance behind him. But by no span of distance could he outrun Gryth's face.

He fled for a long while before he stopped to think where he was going. Only then did the full meaning of this day's work strike him. In running from judgment, he was running from his whole world. From everything. Toward nothing.

For the first time in many hours, he thought of Llyndreth and Angborn and Etheryll to wonder if they had made it through the tunnel.

If not, he had lost all he ever prized for nothing.

Having no other plan, he turned toward the Solgant camp. With him, he took all he now possessed. A knife, a leather coil, and the memory of his brother's face, bleeding a little as Gryth lay against a rock.

10

THE WANING MOON GAVE LIGHT ENOUGH AND MORE AS ZORN peered down into the Solgant camp. The men slept mostly in the open, he noted, though there were some few hide tents scattered here and there. For the lordings, no doubt. It was the way of the Solgants to give special privilege to the highborn. Not so among his own people, he thought with pride; among the Shadow Warriors all lived equal. Then a great sickness swept over him. What need had he for pride, he who no longer belonged?

He dragged his tired mind back to the business at hand. The camp was sleeping, and the girl was like to be inside a tent. He could not find Angborn's vast bulk, but the giant had shaped himself small for entering the tunnel, was apt to be so yet. Zorn's gaze moved to the horse pens, but he could not pick out the one small, brown-dappled pony that interested him.

For that, he would have to move closer. But not just yet. Leaning his head against a soft-furred arm, Zorn let his weariness go in one great, heaving sigh. He had not slept for more than two days and nights. He had lain still, it was true, while Guroc held him prisoner, but his troubled thoughts had given him little peace. This night he must rest.

Tomorrow, as early as might be, he would make sure of his friends' safety. It would be good to look on the girl again before he left, though from a distance and unannounced. And then he would go on. Just where, he was not sure; nor in his exhaustion did it seem to matter much. To a place, wherever it might be, that held neither Solgants nor Danturi. To a place where he was not dishonored.

He was jerked roughly from the depths of sleep. Half awake, he struggled instinctively against brawny Solgant arms. But there were many arms, how many he could not guess, with great, mauling fists at the end of them; and his knife, or rather Gryth's, was gone.

He was slammed to the ground, then hauled upright, Solgant fingers biting into his arms. Mayhap the time was past, he thought groggily, for puzzling where he might go. Mayhap the Solgants would end his wanderings before they rightly started.

They were gabbling in their ugly, uncouth tongue, and what Solgant he had learned along the way had wholly deserted him. Save one word only. He understood the meaning of *goblin* well enough.

They might not, it seemed, kill him just now. They were disputing about that very point, he thought. More than once, he believed he heard the name of Llyndreth's brother, Rothwyn.

Then it was settled, and they were binding him again—he who two days ago had never known the touch of a thong—and with Danturin leather, too, which he had carried with him. They made a great jest of that, holding it close to his face and laughing.

After the knots were secure came the dragging. His own people had brought him tethered as a matter of business, to see that he did not escape. For the Solgants, it was sport instead. There were shouts of "Goblin! Goblin!" and stones thrown his way, most of which he managed to dodge. But the dodging brought forth jeers—there was a taunting note to the unfamiliar words—and it came to him presently that he would bring disgrace upon his people. After that, he dodged no more.

All the while they were moving, he supposed, toward the Solgant camp, though he had no longer any idea of speed or distance. And then they stopped for more arguing. Zorn's nostrils pinched against the smell of horse dung, and somewhere, dimly, he heard a pony whinny. But he was past looking for Etheryll now.

There was one great, loud-voiced brute of a Solgant who did not want him brought into camp, and at last the fellow had his way. Zorn's other captors moved back into a circle, while the one came forward, smiling an ugly, eager smile and pushing back his sleeves.

They had the grace to slip Zorn's bonds, at least, and he understood that he was to make a fight of it. Well, he had not yet held back from a fight, however unequal. The Solgant looked near as big as the Eodan, yet the Danturi knew a trick or two. Once he and Gryth together had . . .

Crouching to defend himself, Zorn winced inwardly. He would have to stop thinking of his spear brother at time of need. Hereafter, all his fights would be alone. . . .

There was an uproar of noise. It came from somewhere near the horse pens. The lord Rothwyn, with his sister in tow, strode angrily toward the shouting. Some quarrel, he supposed. Day by day, his men grew more quarrelsome. Small wonder, too, for nothing had turned out as they expected. You could not attack an enemy you could not find, and the Danturi had proved as elusive as the shadows they named themselves after.

"It is a wolf without teeth," cried a harsh, mocking voice, "though it snarls well enough."

"Hold!" snapped the lord Rothwyn, pushing through the edges of the crowd. "What business is afoot here?"

Some few heads turned. Some few shouts died to a mutter. "Scum!" the voice at the center of the circle continued. "Goblin scum! Give me a fight, at least."

It was Eldgard as usual, Rothwyn saw with disgust. A born troublemaker, that one. In the dust at Eldgard's boot toes, a furry figure, slight as a boy next to the Solgant's bulk, got slowly to its feet. Unsteadily, it came erect, threw its head back, and spat deliberately in Eldgard's face.

In the moment before Eldgard's roar of fury, Rothwyn's sister made a small, startled noise. She clutched at his sleeve.

"Zorn," she breathed. "It's Zorn. Stop them, Rothwyn!"

Without waiting for an answer, she went plunging into the circle, shoving past his soldiers as though she were ten feet tall.

The Danturin was on the ground again, Eldgard's boot drawn back for a kick.

But Llyndreth, her feet planted firmly, faced Eldgard above the crouching form. "Do that," she said in a quiet, taut voice, "and see how you shall pay. By my father's bones but you shall pay!"

It was odd, Rothwyn thought, that she should swear by their father. For she looked like him now. She had his warrior look about her, the hard, stubborn tilt to her jaw, the glitter of frost-on-flint in her gray eyes. And always before he had thought her gentle!

Eldgard lowered his boot and drew back a step or two. He looked to Rothwyn for support. "It is only a goblin, my lord," he said, handing Rothwyn Zorn's knife. "The boys and I were bringing him to you, but we thought first to have a little fun. To let him learn what it is to spy on Solgants."

Llyndreth swept the ring of soldiers with her gaze. "Solgants!" She hurled the word at them. "Solgant warriors! A proud day, is it not, when the lot of you together can conquer one Danturin!"

Her goblin was sitting up. He was a sorry sight, his leather garments ripped and dusty. Blood dripped from a wicked gash above one temple; the other eye was swelling shut. Yet the remaining eye shone savage and defiant. A goblin eye, thought Rothwyn, in a face from old Gryff's nightmare stories. He was not sorry his men had taken away the knife.

If Llyndreth remembered the tales, she did not show it. She held her hand out to the goblin, and her face was no warrior's now but a girl's again. Almost, she seemed about to cry.

"Rothwyn," she demanded, "send someone to bring me water."

It came to him that she meant to tend the creature herself. In a moment she would be on her knees in the dust with half his Solgant host looking on. Lord of Light, but she must not do that!

The goblin had refused her hand. There was that to be grateful for. The lord Rothwyn stepped forward and put his arm around his sister's shoulder. "Let be, Llyndreth," he said. "He will be well cared for. I promise."

"But he is my friend. It is for me to—"

"My own healer will tend to him," said Rothwyn, "but not you. You must not forget what he is." He turned to Eldgard. "Look you, the Danturin is under my protection. I will charge you with it and hold you guilty if you fail. Keep watch over him, but do not harm him. Let no man do him hurt in this camp."

He led Llyndreth away, past the horse pens. She came slowly, reluctantly, but she did come.

Behind them, in the dizzy sunlight of midmorning, the Danturin struggled to his feet.

*　*　*

It was growing dusk when Llyndreth came to Zorn's tent.
Dimly, he heard her voice disputing with the guard outside.
He did not want to see her. She was Solgant, all Solgant, and
he had felt over-many Solgant fists about him that day. They
had waked in him the foe-fury that had dimmed along the
trail.

He did not answer when first she called his name. But she
refused to go away. She stood, light flickering golden around
her, and held her ground. "I grieve for your ill greeting,
Zorn," she said. "How do you? Are you much hurt?"

And because his worst hurt of all was loneliness, he tried
to forget once more that she was Solgant.

"I'm whole enough," he said gruffly, though he ached in
bone and muscle and battered eye. "Knocked about a little.
Nothing worth weeping over."

It was well he thought so, for she did not weep. Nor come
close to see his bruises for herself, as she might have done
along the trail.

"If you lack for anything . . ."

She could scarce give back his honor or his spear brother.
"Na," he said. "Nothing."

"I did not think to see you here, Zorn. What if your people
should find out?"

The shame burned hot inside him. Was it not enough that
she had seen him in the dust with a Solgant boot toe in his
ribs? Must he tell her also that he was outcast and dishonored?

"They can spare me this little while," he muttered. "I came to learn how you fared in the tunnel."

She shivered a little, remembering. But the Danturin priest-kind had been overfearful of the Old Ones' magic, or else Zorn's binding spell had proven stronger than he'd hoped.

"Nothing disturbed us," she said, "save for fallen rocks. And the way was plain enough, despite its twisting and turnings. We could see where other paths had led once, but they were all sealed off.

"It was a dead place, though, a *shuddery place*, dark as the bottom of a well and twice as musty."

There was loathing in her voice. Zorn felt lonelier, somehow, then he had before her coming.

"Where is the Old Man of the Forest?" he asked hurriedly.

"Gone home, soon as might be." Llyndreth smiled. "Glad to be rid of me, I'd wager. He is unused to wayward girls and likes spiders better.

"He left me a gift, though." She stretched out her right arm proudly. "It is old, so old that even Angborn knows little of its story. But he wore it round his wrist as a boy until it grew too tight."

Llyndreth laughed. "It's too large for me, however high I wear it. I must forever keep pushing at it, but I shall wear it always. It's worth a good deal of shoving to own a thing that has belonged to giants."

Zorn peered at the circlet with his good eye. No bright bauble, certainly. Old, old indeed, and dull. But the fine, del-

99

WASHINGTON MIDDLE SCHOOL LIBRARY
Olympia, Washington

icate pattern worked into its metal band gnawed somehow at his memory. Like a thing seen so long ago that you cannot be sure it was ever real. Or one seen so often that it has grown invisible. He felt a foolish desire to touch it.

"It has a Danturin look," he muttered. Which was pure nonsense. Why would old Angborn have owned a Danturin arm ring?

Llyndreth drew her arm away at that as though he'd laid claim to her treasure. "Angborn said it might be a thing of power and that I must be careful of it. He said it was a mark of trust, his parting with it at all."

Suddenly she was anxious to leave. "I disobeyed Rothwyn to come here," she said. "He would be very angry if he knew."

She rose and stood in the doorway, hesitating. "You will be leaving soon, I suppose, lest your people miss you. Send me some word of it. Let Rothwyn think what he will, I shall not let you go without farewell." She looked down, shamefaced. "I cannot come again till then."

So he was now taboo to her, not to be touched or sought out. Else her brother would be angry.

"No need to trouble the lording by farewells," he said harshly. "I shall go of a sudden when my mind turns to it and have small time for leave-taking."

She looked for a moment as if she might protest. Then her face went hard and white, and she left the tent in silence.

She did not come again.

* * *

Etheryll rubbed her head against Zorn's chest, hoping for a treat. "Na," he told the pony, feeling the horse master's eyes upon him from a distance, "I've nothing for you now. Treats come in the morning only." He grinned sourly, thinking that the horse master must lose much sleep rising before dawn to watch him. Did the fool think he would steal the whole herd of Solgant ponies?

It was for no such purpose that he came, certainly. When he went away, he would go on foot as always. If he came to the horse pens each morning before first light, it was only to visit Etheryll—and to enjoy the last good moments before the loud, cramped camp awoke.

Afterward, the whole mountain shuddered, almost, at the Solgants' tramping and shouting, the stamping of their horses, the blare of their accursed horns. It was an ache in him, the noise, almost as bad as the blinding sunlight.

He had come now, toward evening, because he needed to think. He could sort his thoughts out better here among the horses, where he met with no hostility. The Solgant animals, at least, had learned to accept him.

Not so the men. No one struck him anymore nor spat on him, for the lord Rothwyn had given orders. But accidents happened when he was not quite careful. A booted Solgant leg beneath his feet by magic. A brawny shoulder wheeling against him when he found it necessary to eat. And eyes that cried "goblin" when Solgant lips did not.

Twice now, in halting, laborious Solgant, he had asked for his knife back. Twice now, the lord Rothwyn had spoken him fair, yet he still had no knife. And he was always watched. He knew now, beyond doubt, that Llyndreth's brother meant to keep him prisoner. Let him try, then, the vainglorious Solgant lord. Let Rothwyn learn how many drowsy, night-blind guards were needed to keep a Shadow Warrior from melting into shadows.

He would leave when he chose, no mistaking of it, and he would have his knife back when he went. And it would be soon. . . .

So Zorn promised himself each day. Yet it was none so easy, he was finding, to set out for nowhere, in search of nothing. He was not afraid of danger. It was the great lonely emptiness that stalled him. . . .

There was this, too. Llyndreth was sister to a fool. Because the Danturi had lain quiet, watching, and had not struck, the lord Rothwyn was growing easy in his mind. Did he think the Shadow Warriors would wait till their mountain sprouted Solgant towers?

Zorn knew what they awaited, if Rothwyn did not. They would strike, most certainly, in the dark of the moon. If they took their enemy unaware, there would be an end to Solgants on this mountain. An end to him if he were still here.

And to Llyndreth. He had brought her to this camp at the cost of his whole world. He had brought her to the end of everything.

So Zorn watched the waning moon and lingered. And told himself that he needed no one, that he could do well enough on his own, that in time the loneliness would ease.

It was a brave-making boast only. He faced that now, with

his fingers tangled in Etheryll's mane as the pony nuzzled at his chest.

The disdain of Rothwyn's soldiers could not hurt him overmuch. He could even shut his mind sometimes, if he tried hard enough, to the loss of his honor. But Guroc's malice and the breaking of his spear bond with Gryth—those were hurts that festered within him like raw, untended wounds.

As never before, he needed someone to talk to.

It would have to be Llyndreth. There was no one else.

He had been a fool not to tell her the truth at first. It was the brave-making tales that did it. And the sneaking, cowardly fear that, busy with her own kind, she would care little for a Danturin's troubles.

But perhaps it was not that she hadn't cared. Nor even that Rothwyn's orders had kept her away. Perhaps it had been his own ungracious, stiff-necked pride.

Well, he would remedy all that. He would tell the girl the whole unchancy truth, as once he might have done with Gryth. And she would care. Almost, he was sure she would. Then he would warn her of the danger.

Zorn felt better already as he set off to find her. With one friend left, things could not be altogether hopeless.

Llyndreth was not at her tent. Nor was she near the cook pots, where the evening's meal was under way. Zorn walked the whole camp without finding her. When she finally did appear, he stopped short, cursing his luck.

She had been for a walk with Threlgar, her brother's second in command. The two strolled into camp side-by-side, so deep in conversation that Zorn scarcely needed to step back beside the corner of a tent.

He did so, nonetheless. The last thing he wanted was to face Threlgar. The fellow, who scarcely troubled to hide his scorn for goblins, put Zorn severely out of sorts.

Like enough, he could cure that contempt if ever they met in battle! Zorn was savoring the idea, with a sort of grim pleasure, when the word *goblin* drifted around the corner.

He had not meant to listen. In truth, he could understand few Solgant words when they came tumbling one after the other. But the term *goblin* touched him very nearly.

Threlgar said it again and something about an "ugly creature" too.

Zorn stood rigid, waiting for the girl's reply. He caught only the Solgant word for "friend" at first. It was what he had wanted to hear. He relaxed a little.

But she went on more slowly, hesitating. ". . . am not easy with him." Zorn was puzzling that out, stumbling over the word *easy*, when *goblin* struck him again. He had not thought to hear it from her lips. And then "makes me shudder." He knew of *shudder*, somewhat. She had used that Solgant word for the black terror of the tunnel. It was a word of fear and loathing.

So he was a goblin yet and ugly, and he made her shudder. Perhaps she was shuddering now at the mere thought of him.

Zorn did not wait to hear more.

* * *

How he got to the edge of camp, he could not afterward have told. But he sat down on a flat rock and gazed blindly across the valleys below.

It was just as well, he told himself, to know exactly what people thought of you. You were less apt, that way, to make a fool of yourself.

Not that he had imagined Llyndreth admired him. In truth, he had never stopped to think how he might look to her. *Though certain Danturin girls thought him quite handsome.* Na. He had been too busy breaking taboos and fighting his friends for her sake to consider that.

It was no great wonder if she found him strange looking. But to say he made her shudder ... and to Threlgar! If that was friendship among the Sun-Spawned, then he would have to do without a friend.

His going was settled, at least. The when of it, if not the where. There was nothing to hold him here past full darkness and a chance at his knife.

He sat long, scarcely noticing the shadows lengthening into dusk. And if his heart ached more than was proper for a Shadow Warrior, only the darkness knew it. For he was quite alone.

11

CLOAKED IN THICK DARKNESS, ZORN LOOKED OUT AT THE DISTANT mountains that marked the boundary of his particular world.

Free again! He breathed deep of the feeling and then, reminding himself that freedom was a joy he meant to cling to, flattened himself more cautiously against the cliff wall.

That ridge of jagged peaks. No warrior among the Danturi had ever tried to go there. It would be no easy venture. First, one must cross a wasteland of black and tortured rock where no thing grew, not one sprig of green nor hardy, struggling thornbush.

What lay past that barrier, he could not begin to guess. Only death, perhaps, and loneliness. But it would be death without dishonor. And loneliness without the false hope of friendship.

Above all, the mountains were the farthest place he knew from Solgant lands. That was enough, and more than enough, for him.

He would set out at dawning. He stood a better chance of

hiding from the Solgants by day than from his own people at night. Such traveling would not be so bad. Though he still found the wicked glare of midday near unbearable, he had learned to endure the shadowed light of early morn and waning afternoon. You could stand almost anything, he supposed, if your need was great enough.

But just now he needed a refuge from the Danturi till they fled the coming light. It was not merely Guroc's party he must dodge now. Long since the hunt cry would have been sounded against him. He would be a prize for any Shadow Warrior the whole height and breadth of the mountain. A royal prize, coveted by king and king's heir alike.

He knew where he might hide. No one, not even Gryth or Guroc, would come seeking him in the taboo passageways of the Forgotten Ones. But the idea chilled him. To be sure, he had stepped inside, just barely, to speak a binding spell before he sent his companions into the tunnel. No one had known, nor ever would, how much those steps had cost him. It did not reassure him greatly that the girl and the Eodan had come through safely. They were not Danturi. For them there was no taboo.

When Zorn had looked on those half-sealed doors in boyhood, he had thought himself brave enough to try their terrors. He knew himself better now that the need of doing so was on him. Rather, he would face a whole army of icaranths than to cross such a threshold into the unknown. The icaranths belonged, at least, to his own world.

But if there was safety anywhere on the mountain for an attainted traitor, it lay in the taboo places. And the priest-kind, whom he had already offended, had their own magic. Could the Forgotten Ones be so much worse?

Zorn drove himself toward a forbidden passage. Not to the tunnel his companions had passed through—that one would be watched now, surely, or else sealed fresh and tight by order of High Priest Hrald.

Instead, he climbed to another, higher up the side of the mountain, one he remembered from his boyhood ramblings. An easy climb, it was—deadly if his spear brothers should spot him. The entry hole was grown over with brush now, and the brambles tore at him, as if in warning, while he stripped the opening free.

He was trembling when the way was finally clear. He mocked himself nervously. What fright figure did he expect to find inside? Hrald the Old, with his hood and sacred smoke, to accuse him of breaking the ancient law? That was the fate he meant to escape by entering.

The mockery did little to hearten him. There was only one way to enter: a blind, unthinking plunge inside, shutting your mind to old Hrald and whatever lay inside, letting your feet and legs take you past where your courage stopped short, muttering the strongest binding spell you knew as you rushed in.

So Zorn found himself inside the corridor. He scrambled along, not allowing himself to stop and think, until he stumbled at last over an unseen, shattered rock. He lay still then, where he had tripped, waiting to get the feel of the place. He remembered what Llyndreth had told him about the other tunnel: *a dead place. Dark as the bottom of a well, and musty.*

Well, it was dark, certainly. A rather pleasant dark in Zorn's opinion. And musty, too, but no mustier than other places he had been in. He was not sure about its being dead. There was something about the place, a vague something— no more, perhaps, than the dread raised in him by his own priest-kind—that whispered of power.

He sat up, because he felt less vulnerable sitting, and thought about what he had gotten into. He was not so afraid now. It was not so bad a place, actually. Much better than he had dared to hope for after all the disheartening things that had happened to him lately. Even if the power he felt was real and not in his mind only, it did not seem threatening. But it was enough to make him cautious.

Easing back against the wall, he made himself comfortable and wondered about the Forgotten Ones. Who had they been, and whither had they vanished? Had the mountain been a kinder place when they had dwelt there?

He sat motionless for a long time, watching, listening. But there was nothing to disturb the silent stillness. The tunnel might have been empty for a thousand years, yet from some-where, deep within his mind, Zorn still felt dim stirrings of life. Of power.

It was, however, a thing you grew used to. A thing like the whisper of water in a stream, so faint you scarcely noticed it, so steady that it came to soothe you.

It became wearisome, watching against emptiness, listen-ing against silence. And a sense of peace grew on Zorn. For the first time in a very long while, he had had neither Solgant nor Danturin enemies to worry over.

In time, he dozed.

Waking, he hurried to the door of the tunnel and found with dismay that it was nearly dusk. How could he have slept the whole day through? No time now to make his descent from the mountain. He would be lucky to find food before nightfall.

Entering was much easier the second time. He scarcely gave a thought to Hrald and the other priest-kind. It was as though he had found a door to another world where his dishonor and Guroc's betrayal, even the loss of Gryth and Llyndreth, faded to nothing.

He had no need of sleep now. He was stiff from too much sitting, and curiosity overmastered him. Cautiously at first, then with a sort of restless eagerness, Zorn began to explore the tunnel. He tramped for some while—pausing now and again to watch and listen, feeling a little foolish afterward at the emptiness that invariably met his watchfulness—when the tunnel unexpectedly branched off in two directions.

Zorn stopped to consider. Had he not best turn back? There was no commonsense way to choose between the corridors. Taking either was as much a gamble as guessing which of Gryth's knotted fists contained a pebble.

It was the memory of Gryth as much as anything that decided Zorn. He could not bear to sit idle until sunrise. He did not want so much time for thinking.

For no particular reason, he picked the right-hand passage. It led on and on, quiet and empty and monotonous. Zorn half wished he'd not come at all. His belly rumbled a new complaint. Perhaps he could have napped if he'd lain still. It was a hard trip, cruelly hard, that he was planning. He'd need all the strength rest could bring him when once he tried crossing the wasteland.

And then slowly, little by little, Zorn found that the sense of power he'd felt within the tunnel was growing stronger. It weighed on him like some heavy boulder. He caught himself fingering his knife—as though this was something a knife could ward against.

The knife was useless, of course, against a thing you could neither see nor hear. He put it away.

Zorn would have turned back gladly now, but he had come too far entirely to play coward.

The corridor snaked suddenly so that you could not see what came next. Yet you could feel. . . . He had to force himself to round the corner into that place of power.

He stopped short, amazement giving way to weak-kneed, foolish relief. He was no stranger to this place! It was the Cave of Warrior Making. Like every other boy who would join the Shadow Warriors, he had spent a day and a night alone within this place.

It was a place of power, to be sure. That was why the boys were sent here, to test their courage. But there was no magic here he had not endured before.

And yet . . .

The smothering sense of helplessness was still with him. He had not felt like this before!

Then the wrongness struck him. He had crawled inside a

taboo tunnel. He had walked the length of it, knowing it belonged to the Forgotten Ones. And it had brought him to a Danturin priest-place.

He found that more sinister, somehow, than if he had found—found what? He did not know, after all, what he had thought to find. And he was being very foolish. He should be glad that he had come to a known, familiar place. And more than glad that it was not the time of warrior making, when he might have walked straight into Old Hrald's arms.

But the cave still fretted him. He did not like to think he was afraid, but it was no wisdom for a traitor to linger in a cave the priest-kind claimed. Mayhap they knew when an intruder came. . . .

Zorn had no wish to leave by the path the boy warriors used. He searched the place thoroughly, as he had not done when he became a warrior. He had been too busy with his dreams then, he thought with a pang. Dreams of his own bravery and of the glory he would win as a warrior.

There were, he found, three doors to the cave. The one by which he had entered from the tunnel, the one that the Danturi used, and yet a third, sealed by a great slab of stone.

He did not like the looks of this last. It had been long and long since the slab was moved; it had weathered to the exact look of the surrounding walls so that it took a careful eye, and something of luck as well, to discover it. And it was here, near the slab, Zorn discovered, that the sense of his helplessness weighed most heavily on him.

He moved away quickly. Already, he had tampered with too many taboo things.

He found at last the thing he looked for. It was a hole in the cave wall, no bigger than he needed to crawl through, and offering no view to the outside either. But he felt fresh air against his cheek and knew, with a gratitude so sharp it was painful, that he had found a private way out.

He lost no time. Muttering a charm, he wriggled through the hole and came presently into a much smaller cave. The air was better here. And the sense of power was gone. Zorn rose, stretched himself, and stepped stiffly to the edge of the cave. It was night, what night he was scarcely sure. It seemed to him that he had been in the tunnel and the Cave of Warrior Making forever.

The wind felt cool and good, but it brought with it a warning. He caught the smell of Solgant and Danturi, mingled together, and along with it something else too. The raw odor of new-slain flesh.

There was a thin fragment of moon left, the last splintered shard of the last quarter. So the Hunter's Dark was not quite come. But Myrgg had struck early.

There was unrest on the whole mountain. It rode on the night air, bristling the short, smooth fur along the back of Zorn's neck. The rocks quivered with it for those who knew how to feel, and the war rhythms danced in Zorn's own blood.

What had happened to the girl?

It was not his to care. He was a goblin. And an outcast. And no friend to any Solgant.

It—was—not—his—to—care.

12

IT WAS NOT YET DARK ENOUGH FOR SAFETY, BUT ZORN DARED WAIT no longer. The cover of darkness he had always relied on would bring still worse perils.

Once again, as he had already half a hundred times this night, Zorn cursed his stupidity. He should have been in the faraway, dim foothills by now. There—or lost forever in the jagged rocks between.

Instead, he had circled back to the Solgant camp. Because he had no firmness of purpose. Because he was forever a fool.

Not that it was sympathy for the girl that had brought him back. It was simply that he had lost so much on her account. He could not bear that it should all go for nothing.

He had feared yesternight, when he came forth from the cave, that it might have ended so already. But the camp still stood.

King Myrgg—Zorn grinned despite himself—there was a guileful leader. This long while he had kept his warriors hidden so that the Solgants grew restless and cocky and over-eager. Then, as the moon shrank away to nothing, he had sent out raiding parties to harass Rothwyn's soldiers so that they grew hungry for Danturin blood. Rothwyn—the fool—had taken the bait. He had split his force to follow the raiders, leaving his camp but ill-protected.

And this night fell the Hunter's Dark. . . .

Long ago the Danturi had mastered the art of creeping. They had learned it from their brothers, the small hunted animals of the earth. Tonight it stood Zorn in good stead.

He came soundlessly to Llyndreth's tent, slipped soundlessly beneath the flap. Her back was to him. She was combing her hair, the long, sun-colored hair that he had once found ugly. It shone from the little winking flame-in-a-jar that Solgants use.

He should stop her mouth lest she call out in alarm. But it was taboo to touch a Solgant. Her hair fell soft and bright as the comb swept through it.

If she made any outcry, he was lost. But he must not, dared not, touch her.

"Rothwyn's sister," he said very softly, "let you make no noise."

She turned and her head came up. There was nothing in her face, neither fear nor welcome; and she spoke as quietly as he did. "Why have you come?"

"I have come to warn you. Tonight the Danturi will attack this camp."

It was as if she had not heard him. "To warn me. And yet you did not even say farewell."

Dantur's Bones! After all that he had endured, she was

trying to put him in the wrong! " 'Twould have been a goblin's farewell," he said. "Like enough it would have made you shudder."

Her eyes widened with surprise. "I never said such—"

"Na. To me, you did not. But to the lording Threlgar."

Her face went scarlet and furious. "So you listened by stealth, from the shadows. I have often heard that the Danturi were sneaks and skulkers. I had never believed it of you till now."

Let him keep good hold on his temper. He had known better than to look for friendship or gratitude from her. He had not come for that. And there was no time to lose by quarreling.

"Sa," he agreed stiffly. "It is always so with goblins. They will sneak and skulk and attack by the dark of the moon. It is so tonight, also. Let you see that their skulking is not the death of you."

This time she did pay attention. The angry color drained from her face, leaving it pale and tense. "Are you sure of it? Then I must give warning."

Zorn almost laughed. "Let you do so by all means. Tell my lord Threlgar that the goblins are coming. Tell him that a goblin told you. Will he make ready his defenses on my word, think you? 'We give you thanks, good goblin, for your warning.'"

Llyndreth did not answer. Another thought had come to her. "You should not have come. It must be dangerous for you. If your people should find out—"

"They do not know. But Threlgar will know when once

116

you tell him. Shall I tell you what he will do? He will laugh behind his hand that you were so foolish as to believe a goblin. And me, he will take captive as a spy. He will bind me fast, as your brother never chose to do. And there will be no escaping for either of us."

"But what else can I do?" Llyndreth demanded. "I cannot run away, leaving my people in danger."

"Can you not? You are no warrior, surely. How shall it help your brother's soldiers if you stay? Will it cheer Lord Rothwyn if he returns to find your corpse alongside theirs?"

"I cannot go. You must see that. I cannot desert my people.

"But I will say nothing to Threlgar till you are gone. I give you thanks for your warning. I would not have it bring you trouble."

He might have known that she would cast her Solgant honor at him when his own was lost beyond reclaiming.

"Na," he said bitterly. "You would not bring me trouble. Yet when day next dawns, you will be dead. And all of it will be for nothing."

It was more than he had meant to say. She was staring at him, the comb dangling, all forgotten, in her hand. "All of it? What will all be for nothing?"

He shook his head. "Let you decide if you will come."

Llyndreth studied him sharply. "You could not have slipped away this night unmissed. Not just before an attack. If ever you had been with your fellow warriors . . ."

She went on, speaking not to him but to herself. "You found no welcome in our camp, and yet you stayed and stayed. I wondered why you didn't return to your own people. It was because you could not, wasn't it? Even then you could not. And because of me."

"It is past changing, Sun's Daughter. And it was not your fault."

He saw that, suddenly, with miserable clarity. He had come here this night as one who claimed a debt. But there was no debt. She had never asked that he break oath with his people, had never asked that he should put her first. He had made his own choice when he did that.

If she wished to die with her own kind, he could scarce protest. Had she not her own right of choosing?

He took a backward step toward the tent flap. The flame-in-a-jar threw golden glints on her long, unbound hair.

"Fortune shield you, Sun's Daughter," he said, moving heavily. Fortune would not shield her. Nothing could if she stayed here. She would never see another sunrise. She would see death instead, or else the dark halls of Dantur.

And for him, a bright, blind emptiness of days—

Llyndreth's voice caught him at the doorway. "Wait a moment, Zorn," she said low-spoken, "while I clothe me warmly." She had turned round in her mind, though the turning of it was a mystery to him. "There is my brother's second-best bow I must find, too, and arrows for it. We may need weapons to win beyond the mountain."

LLYNDRETH HUDDLED SPIRITLESSLY AGAINST A BOULDER. NEVER had she been so spent. Every part of her was stiff and aching—arms, legs, shoulders. Even her feet were bruised and bleeding.

"Sa," Zorn said with approval. "You have made a climb few Solgants would have dared. It is a thing to take pride in."

She did not want to be proud. She wanted only to forget the terror of her night-blind, torturous scramble upward. She had been afraid every instant since Zorn had left the pony concealed in a deep cleft and had told her what he meant to do.

She felt his gaze on her now. "It will be easier for you inside the mountain." he said. "It is an easy path, going downward always. There will be no need to climb."

Inside the mountain? Resentment flared inside her. He did not know how much she feared the darkness. Did not know what she had suffered already, climbing blindly, groping for unseen footholds, clutching desperately at the furry hand he reached down for her. How could he, who was so surefooted, begin to know the sick panic of rock slipping away beneath your feet?

Or perhaps he did know. He had left the Solgant camp because he was angry with her. Perhaps he was glad of her misery and helplessness—

"Come now," Zorn said urgently. "You may rest once you are in the tunnel." She remembered what a tunnel was like. Oh, yes, she remembered excellently well. The stifling darkness, shut off from sun and air and even stars. On the hillside just now, there had at least been wind and stars.

"We need not go inside," she begged. "They'll not think to look for us up here."

"Not search, na. Yet they might find us by mischance. In the tunnel lies safety."

Icaranths also, perhaps. And repulsive crawling things she could not name. And the fear within herself of being trapped.

"I'll not go inside," she said in a small, stiff, stubborn voice.

"Will you not?" He sounded as though he did not care in the least. "I must go down alone, then, to hide your pony. And when your brother returns, he will pass far beneath, close by the tunnel's lower opening. But you will not be there."

Her fear exploded into anger. "If you wanted us down below, why did you make me climb and climb—"

"Because my spear brothers"—he corrected himself—"because the Shadow Warriors are great hunters. Had we entered below, they would have found your hiding place straightaway. But now we have left no trail leading into the cave. Assuredly, they will pass it by. When I have taken the pony, its tracks, too, will lead them from your door."

Llyndreth supposed he was right. He sounded very logical and patient. But the thought of the tunnel tightened around her, as if already it cut her off from light and freedom. "I cannot," she whispered. "I would rather face the Danturi than be shut up inside the mountain."

"Sa?" Zorn's eyes gleamed in the dark, catlike. "You would rather face the Danturi? Think you it comes so easy, then, to stand alone among those who scorn you? How long could you endure to be spit upon by—by goblins?"

He stopped short. When he spoke again, his voice was harsh, as though the words hurt in the speaking. "And yet, already, you are with a goblin."

Not that. That was not what she feared at all. "Oh, no. But who knows what kind of creatures live inside the mountain? Slimy, crawling things, mayhap. Or"—a fresh horror struck her—"there may even be bats."

"Bats?" Zorn echoed the word blankly. Then he began to laugh. There was a young sound to his laughter, young and carefree. Llyndreth had never before heard him laugh, had not been sure the Danturi ever did laugh.

When peal after peal had died away, he sat on his heels still rocking helplessly. "Bats," he said finally. "So it is bats you fear more than the fiercest Shadow Warriors. Guroc would be ill-flattered.

"I can shield you from bats," he promised. "Yes, and from

your slimy creatures too." For an instant he hesitated, then held out his hand. "Come," he said simply. "I will let no beast come near you, even."

It was no Solgant hand that gripped hers. It was too furry for that, by far. But it was tight and strong and comforting. And Zorn had sounded boyish, laughing beside her. No different, after all, from Rothwyn or Eathrydd.

She came to her feet that he might lead her, blind, into the heart of the mountain.

He let her stop presently. It was the first time she'd really rested since they left the Solgant camp. Or had a chance to think.

It was Zorn she thought of. What lay ahead if he was outcast from his people?

Timidly, she voiced her thoughts. "Where will you go, Zorn, after this night?"

"There are other mountains beyond this one."

She shuddered. She knew the bleak, empty-looking peaks he meant. And the wasteland between.

If she might ask him to go with her— But both knew what he might look for among her people. He would want no more of Solgant kindness.

She herself had hurt him. She could try, at least, to make amends for that. "Zorn," she began hesitantly, "let you listen to me. The things you heard me say that day—to Threlgar—"

"Na." The rock she sat on was no harder than his voice. "We'll not talk of that."

"But if you will hear me out—"

Zorn rose abruptly. "Must you needs remind me what a fool I am? I need no reminding of it."

"Zorn, please—"

He was moving silently down the corridor, leaving her to grope after him as best she could. Llyndreth hardened her heart against him. If he would not let her ask his pardon, let him think what ugly thing he chose.

But she missed the comfort of his hand on hers.

They walked long and long before he spoke again. "The tunnel ends here," he said curtly. "There's one cave and then—" He stopped short.

Llyndreth began to be afraid. "What is it, Zorn?"

"Your arm ring," he said. "We must hurry! This is a place of power, and it is not good to linger."

Llyndreth twisted her neck, peering down at her upper arm. Faintly but unmistakably, the arm ring was glowing with a bluish light.

She drew it downward so that she could see it better. The metal seemed warm against her fingers like a living thing. And it was beautiful. She had never thought it beautiful before.

Zorn seized her arm. "Come," he said. "The hole's over here. Close to the ground. It's a tight squeeze, but—"

Llyndreth broke away. One side of the arm ring was brighter than the other. It glittered like the blue heart of fire.

She was not tired any longer. Her aches and bruises were forgotten. Likewise, her fear of caves. She stripped off the arm ring and held it before her, following the bright side.

Ever the blue glow deepened as she moved. She could see close around her now. Could see Zorn's face in the darkness. "This is an unchancy place," he said. "A priest-place. Already I have broken taboo to bring you here. Let us be gone." There was a pleading note in his voice. She had never known Zorn to plead before.

In her excitement, she ignored it. She had reached the wall now. And in the wall, there was a door. No chance of missing it. Around its edges gleamed the same pale, bluish fire.

"Zorn," she cried, "look you!"

"Sa," he said dryly. "A door sealed for ages past by the priest-kind. Surely they had their reasons. Show some sense and leave it."

Mayhap he was right. But when you own an arm ring that glows with blue fire and shows you passageways . . . Llyndreth pressed against the door.

It was a great rock slab that could never have moved from her slight weight against it. And yet it had. The arm ring glowed still brighter.

"Llyndreth!" Zorn's cry seemed to come from a great distance. "Let you not go through!" There was fear in his voice. Never till now, she knew in the back of her mind, had he called her by her true name.

But just now, there was only the arm ring.

She stood in her own small circle of blue light. Beyond, swirling around her, was all-devouring blackness. She had never seen such blackness. Not in the tunnel, nor struggling up the hillside.

And the dark was terror. She had disobeyed Zorn. Already he was angry with her. What if he stayed behind, as she deserved, and left her to face this blackness alone?

She wanted to turn back now, but her legs were frozen lumps. Her tongue, also, so that she could not call out.

And then she heard Zorn's voice close behind. "I ask your pardon, Solgant," he said with a touch of uncertain laughter. "I thought it was I who did not dread the darkness."

She groped for his hand, and nothing had ever seemed more welcome than his fingers closing over hers.

"Can you see in here?" she asked shakily.

"I was born Danturin, and I have yet the eyes I was born with."

"Then what manner of place is this?"

"A great cave. Like others I have seen, only larger. Much larger." Zorn spoke with awe. "You could put King Myrgg's palace and the Warrior Hall inside it and have room to spare, I think, for the hearth-places of half the Danturi ever born.

"But it is no mere cave either. Because there are tunnels stretching out from it like the rays on your Solgant sun-emblem. And the cave walls are pocked with—well, they are smaller caves, I suppose. I cannot see inside them." He paused uneasily. "I did not think there was a blackness I could not see through."

He did not even try to disguise the fear in his voice. "Can you not feel the power? I promised to protect you, but that was from ordinary things. We have no right to be here. Let you forget that arm ring and leave this unchancy place!"

She did feel it. And she was ready. She had not thought

the blackness would be so terrifying or that she might be dragging Zorn into danger. The sad truth was she had not thought at all.

And then, noiselessly, without warning, the darkness exploded into light. Green fire this time that came spiraling out of nowhere to flash on the roof and walls of the cave and then dance away elsewhere. It might have been lightning, save that lightning was never such a pale, luminous green shot with blue flame that waxed and waned in its midst.

Zorn stumbled backward a step, one hand holding firmly to Llyndreth's, the other shielding his eyes against the pain of dancing light.

But for the girl it was different. Now, for the first time, she saw the cave in all its terrible beauty. The first jagged flash showed her great hourglass portals that might have been hewn by some master mason. It brought gemstones in the wall to green-glittering life. Delicate webs of stone clinging to the ceiling glowed briefly and then disappeared.

Zorn was kneeling now or crouching—she could not tell which, only that he had drawn her down with him to the hard, cool floor. His hand was crushing hers, and she could hear the sound of his ragged breathing.

But then he was chanting. His voice shook at first, then steadied, reaching out into the flaming cave.

> "Dwellers in darkness,
> Keepers of the cave,
> Guardians of the stone
> Both dead and living,

We come in peace.
By Dantur's charm be bound,
And bide you peaceful"

She felt alone, yet somehow neither afraid nor lonely, which was very strange. Strange, too, that in this alien place, while he had drawn apart to work an alien spell, she should feel closer to Zorn than she ever had before. It was as though here in the cave, pitted with him against unknown power, she had felt their differences melt away.

Again and again, hoarsely, Zorn repeated the spell. And slowly, very slowly, the green fire subsided. It burned out to blue, shone softer and less threatening, then flickered out entirely.

The cave was again dark and silent. Zorn neither moved nor spoke. His grip was hurting Llyndreth's hand, and her muscle-weary legs were all cramp and numbness. But perhaps all was not ended though the fire had gone out. Perhaps Zorn was still struggling alone against its power. Perhaps he needed time and quiet and stillness. What did she know of magic?

She tried to be still. She was lonely now and terribly afraid. It was more frightening, somehow, to know that whatever thing they had faced lurked hidden within the cave than to see it in the open. And she was almost sure of what she'd seen in the light of the green fire.

Zorn turned toward her then, loosening his fingers one by one, as though reclaiming them. "I used the strongest binding spell I knew," he said in a drained, dead-weary voice, "the one given to us when we prove ourselves as warriors. But I did not think it would work here. I did not guess it had such power."

She could speak of it now that he had come back. "Zorn," she said, "in one of those dark little chambers, just for a moment, I thought I saw a form. It looked human, almost, only larger."

"It was the stones," he said quickly. "They take strange forms always in a cave. They seem to be a lizard or a throwing spear or even a man. Mostly, it is in the mind."

He had spoken swiftly. Too swiftly and sharper than need be. She was sure now that he had seen it too.

He got to his feet. "Let us make all the haste we can to replace the slab. Such power as we have met is best sealed in the mountain."

It was much easier said than done. The slab, which had swung round so easily coming in, refused to budge going out. Zorn heaved his weight against it from one side, tugged from another, then cleared away imaginary rubble and heaved again. The thing still stood slightly ajar, exactly as it had since first it had opened to let Llyndreth through.

Zorn had sent her ahead into the Cave of Warrior Making, but she groped her way back after a time. "Can I not help? Could not the two of us—"

"Go back and wait," he said curtly. "Let you not stand in the way." She did not know what she was in the way of. He seemed to be staring at the door in baffled annoyance.

He had been angry with her before the arm ring had led them astray. But he could not be out of temper still. Not after what they'd faced together.

"It was I who opened it," she said. "Mine is the blame. Do let me help." And she put her hand to the stone—her right hand with the arm ring above it.

The slab came shut so suddenly that they landed, the both of them, on their backsides in the Cave of Warrior Making.

The door was in place, precisely as they had wanted it. And yet Zorn was muttering in Danturin. "Need you have done that?" he snapped through set teeth. "I almost had it."

That was untrue. He was angry still. Angry and unfair and horrid.

"Did you think," she retorted, "that you had set a binding spell on me that I must do your will?"

"I thought only that you had some sense for a Solgant. Could not Lord Rothwyn's sister bend her will to do as a— to do as I bade you?" He did not wait for an answer but shoved her none too gently in the direction he meant her to go.

He had almost said "goblin" again. She was sick of that hateful word, sicker yet of Zorn's harping on it.

And it was not she who was overproud!

Llyndreth squeezed silently through the hole. It was a horrid hole. Zorn was horrid, too. Most horrid of all was the thought that she might owe him her safety. You can scarce tell someone who has faced an unknown power for you how dreadfully you mislike him.

She was glad, for once, of the cramped quarters that kept

Zorn pinned behind her. One rebellious tear persisted in crawling down the side of her nose. And she had never been quite sure how much a Danturin could see in total darkness.

"Let you not leave this cave," Zorn said, "until I come back. Or until you hear the sound of horses' hooves. The Danturi mislike horses and will not take them. Therefore, hoofbeats will mean your brother's soldiers."

He sounded cool and stiff. They had barely spoken since they entered the passageway.

"There is a pool of good water here, and I have bound the cave creatures to peace. . . ." Zorn's voice trailed off. He stood slowly. "Good fortune shield you, Rothwyn's sister."

It was what he had said long hours ago—could it be hours, only?—when he had thought she would not come with him.

And now, leaving her safe-hidden in the cave, he must go out again. "Zorn," she cried suddenly, "leave the pony be. It may be that they will not find her. Stay here in the cave with me."

"Is it so much to ask that you sit quietly in a cave for a few hours? Your brother is a warrior. Let you try to be brave as a warrior's sister should be."

Nothing he said could make her angry again. Not now, with the thought of his danger fresh in her mind. "It is not for myself I fear. Well, not much, anyway. It's you I'm anxious about. If your people catch you—"

"They cannot." He let himself boast a little, as was a warrior's due. "Not one among the Danturi knows the passage we came by. Nor is there one who knows the hillsides as I do. I have laid claims to cracks and burrows where I could hide from the mountain itself."

Yet he was tired, she knew. As bone-weary as she was, no doubt. It was not enough, suddenly, to wish him good fortune and let him leave the cave unseen, untouched. Groping after his voice, Llyndreth found his hand and seized it. To her surprise, he drew it back, flinching, but she did not let it go. Exploring gently with her fingertips, she found a long, blood-clotted gash along the palm. "You might have told me you were hurt!" she accused. "It was when the slab gave, was it not? You were angry and would not let me help. And then, when you were hurt, you wouldn't even tell me!"

"What could you have done?"

"I could have cared! I could have been sorry!"

Oddly, he did not scoff at that. "It is a small scathe," he said. "Only a scratch, not worth your troubling." But at her bidding, he washed the cut in the cave's pool and let her bind it with a strip from her cloak.

"Since first we met," Llyndreth mourned as she knotted the rag tight, "I have brought you only evil and mischance. If I could give you one better gift at least in leave-taking—"

She straightened abruptly. "And so I shall. Let you take the arm ring. It is not an ill gift. I wore it the whole time. If it had been evil, I would have known it."

"But it is yours. The Eodan meant you to have it."

"He'd not mind. If he'd been here this night, he would be proud."

"Proud to have a goblin wear it, think you? One who makes his friends to shudder?"

"Will you shame me forever, Zorn? When I am trying . . ."
Llyndreth's voice quivered, but Zorn would not break the
silence for her. "Did I hurt you so deep, then," she asked
finally, "that it is past all forgetting? I have tried to ask pardon, and I would give you Angborn's arm-ring. It is all I
have to give."

"I will take it then, Sun's Daughter," Zorn muttered, "since
you wish me to."

She slipped the band round his arm and fastened the clasp.
Then, on an impulse, she touched her lips to his bandaged
hand. He went rigid, and she felt her face heat with the
knowledge that she had done another thoughtless, foolish
thing. "So old Helgydd, my nurse, would do," she stammered,
"when I had hurt myself. She said that kisses heal—"

Then she drew herself up straight. "No, it will heal nothing. But," she said defiantly, "I would not have done so much
for Threlgar. Will you count me friend again and try to forget
my unworthiness?"

Zorn was many moments answering. "I have counted you
friend always," he said at last. "Now I shall remember one
thing only. That you tended my hurt when first we met,
though any other would have counted me enemy."

But almost at once, his voice turned grim and hurried. "I
should have gone long since. Pay heed to all I told you."

He touched her hair in passing. If it was not quite a caress,
still it was no accident. "Bide safe," he said, "friend."

Then Llyndreth was alone in the black and musty silence.

14

SHE HAD SPENT LONG LIFETIMES ENTOMBED IN DARKNESS. LIFE-
times that stretched back beyond the days of Solgant and
Danturin to the all-beginning. She was older than the Eodan,
older than the cave spirits, even, and fear, which was older
yet, lived with her. It skittered with quick, faint footsteps
along the walls of the cave and slithered, belly-smooth, across
the damp stone floor.

The goblin-dread of childhood was with her, too, though
no flame-born shadows danced in the black cave. There were
no goblins, she told herself, only Danturi like Zorn. And
when Zorn had touched her hair in leaving, it had felt light
and gentle, like a caress.

But the shadow goblins leaped and pounced in her mind
nonetheless. They were in pursuit, as they ever had been in
her dreams, and Zorn, who could never again seem goblin,
was their prey.

"I could hide from the mountain itself," he had told her

lightly. But she knew with sick, dismal certainty that he would not hide.

He had with him her pony, Etheryll, which the goblin creatures would be quick to scent. There would be night eyes as keen as his to seek him out. And he would be alone.

Fear, which was older than the all-beginning, skittered along the walls of the cave and slithered, belly-smooth, across the damp stone floor.

Somehow, she had slept at last, for she could not at once remember the source of her fear. She sat up, remembering, and found herself stiff and cramped. Like poor Helgydd, she thought, and it was a new fear finding that Helgydd's face had grown dim and uncertain in her memory.

The cave seemed lighter. She was locked in gloom now, not in blackness. There was a break somewhere, farther back, in the stone roof of the cave through which dim shafts of sunlight came tunneling to reach her. She could have made out forms now if there had been anything to see.

So it was morning. The same sunlight that she found so welcome would have driven the Danturi homeward. Yet Zorn had not returned.

She tried not to think of what that meant.

She would think home thoughts instead. Deliberately, she pictured Helgydd, summoning up each feature till the well-loved whole came clear, conjuring the crinkled, kindly voice that was a perfect match for the face. "Let you have patience, my sunbeam," said the vision. "Let you work your tapestry carefully, that my lord your father may be proud."

But Helgydd's voice trailed off, reshaping itself to the harsher accents of the Common Speech. "Think you the Eodan would want a goblin to wear his arm ring?" it said bitterly.

The hurt behind the words echoed loud through the silent cave.

She should never have come to the mountains. If only she had turned back as Angborn bade her. If she had but gone to stay with Marnne and Eathrydd as she had first thought to do—

Pale broken fragments of sunlight dappled the floor of the cave. Just so, on a long-ago carefree day, they had dappled the loft of her father's barn while she and Marnne bounced, laughing, on great, piled-up heaps of hay. "Be you gentle-born ladies?" Helgydd had scolded fondly, "or mongrel puppies, that you must roll about, getting straw in your hair?" Then she had turned her wrath on Rothwyn and Eathrydd, battling with makeshift wooden swords. "Be you so eager for bruises, young lords," Helgydd had promised, "let you look to your rumps. I shall see to it that you come by your desire!"

It had been a good day, that, despite the scolding, filled with laughter and sharing and love.

Zorn had brought her to a place of safety and gone out, alone, onto the mountain. He had been alone in her brother's camp. Alone. Always alone.

Llyndreth shivered. She had not noticed the chill before, but now the faint, scant light was powerless to warm her. The cave was as cold as a death-place. And empty. Very, very empty.

15

ZORN PULLED REIN AND PATTED THE PONY'S LATHERED NECK. NO use pretending any longer. Etheryll was truly going lame.

He dismounted, gingerly lifted her right foreleg, the one she'd been favoring. Nothing wrong there. It must be her foot fretting her, her "hoof," the Solgants called it. He found the rock almost at once and drew his knife, then hesitated. The stone was deep driven. He was no horse master. If he tried to remove it and failed, he might only make matters worse.

No time for learning now. His plan had gone too well for that. He had drawn the Danturi away from the cave, right enough. They were hard upon his heels.

That should not have mattered. He had had his hiding place picked out, had been confident the Shadow Warriors could not catch him. But now fortune had flown from his shoulder. With the pony lame . . .

Hastily, he scanned the rocks above him. Halfway up the cliff face, or a little more, perhaps, a sharp shelf jutted out. It would serve to shield him—

Etheryll nuzzled uncertainly at his back. He could not take her with him up the steep cliff side. Lame or not, she would have to make a run for it.

He turned and struck without warning. The pony squealed in resentment as the leather thong stung her flank. She burst into an angry trot but slowed after a few yards, halted, and looked back questioningly. If it had been a mistake, she seemed to say, she was willing to give him the benefit of doubt.

Reluctantly, Zorn followed after. He made sure, this time, that the leather cut her sharply; slashed at her rump until she leaped into an awkward run. She was making better time, despite her lameness, now that she carried no burden.

Zorn watched her for a moment. It was an ill way to treat a good companion, one who had carried you and fought beside you. But it was kinder fare than she would get from his spear brothers. Kinder by far than he would get if they laid hands on him.

With the thunder of her hoofbeats in his ear, Zorn began to scale the cliff.

His luck had flown far and far. It would not return this night to sit upon his shoulder. He knew that, scrambling upward, when the first wild notes of keening reached his ears.

The heavy, unfamiliar Solgant bow was a sore hindrance to him. But he would need it when he reached the shelf. His knife would be useless at that distance and he had no spear about him.

The arm ring troubled him too. It chafed between his el-

bow and his shoulder. Let it chafe, then. It was a small price
to pay for having Llyndreth's friendship back. There was a
singing within him for that friendship that not even the
shouts from below could quell.

A spear hummed past him, shattering itself against a rock.
His heart hammering wildly, Zorn shut his eyes against splin-
ters, crawled blindly onward.

Blinking, he saw with relief that the shelf loomed just
ahead. He pulled himself into a favorable position, then
lunged for its shelter to land panting, hungry for breath.

He took precious moments to rest, lying quietly till the
pounding in his chest began to ease, before he heaved himself
onto his stomach and unslung the Solgant bow. He had no
skill with such a weapon. He wondered how much different
it might be from hurling a spear.

You kept your hand steady, he supposed, and your eye
fixed firmly on the target. It was that much like, at least.

He had not wanted to shed Danturin blood, did not want
to now. He had meant to hide, not fight.

But already young Gurd, a new-made warrior, was beginning to work up toward him. Working up without cover. If
he could hit anything at all with an arrow, he could put one
into Gurd. Why did not Gurd's captain call him back to
safety? Zorn willed it so. Call him back, you there below.
Whoever is in command, let you recall him.

But then he heard a voice below, urging Gurd on. He knew
the voice for Guroc's, and hope died. There would be no
calling back this night. Guroc would trade Gurd's blood for
his, rejoicing in the bargain.

They were far below him still. Even Gurd. Zorn was tempted for a moment to climb upward, to try even yet for escape.

But he had not led them so far from Llyndreth's cave as he had wished to. And Guroc was shrewd, wary of being tricked. If they caught the pony and found no Solgant, he might double back. If he once lost Zorn, Guroc would sniff blood out of rock for other prey.

Gurd was coming closer. He must act and act soon. Slowly, Zorn fitted an arrow to the bowstring. He strained, then let the arrow fly. It went winging, winging, and suddenly Gurd was tumbling backward, making an ugly, choking sound and clutching at his chest.

Zorn watched in horror. He had had little notion of hitting Gurd, of hitting anything.

He laid down the bow. His hand was trembling, a sickness rising in his stomach. There had been hope in him yet, he discovered. A feeble, struggling hope that one day he might yet rejoin his people.

Whether Gurd lived or no, that hope had died. Now, in truth, he was oath-broken. He thought of the curse reserved for such as he. "He who turns his spear against his brother . . ."

He looked with loathing at the bow beside him on the rock. Let him steady his hand to lift it, for he would need it soon. Doom clung with sharp claws to his shoulder now, where luck had sat so lightly. The bow would buy him time, time for Llyndreth in the cave.

It was all in the world that was left him.

* * *

From somewhere higher up and to the left of him, he heard the shrill, high-pitched kill-keening of the Shadow Warrior and knew that someone had made his way up the steep slope to come at him from behind. If he could not put an arrow in that climber, he was done.

He was bold, the climber, and arrogant, to sing out his coming when he might have kept silent. He wanted Zorn to know his presence, to feel the shadow of death spread over him. Guroc, perhaps, the fires of his hunt-blood stirred by malice.

Reluctantly, Zorn fitted an arrow to the bow and swerved, his eyes scanning the rocks for any sign of movement, his ears tuned to the fierce, mournful hunt song. His last chance of escape would go flying on this arrow. This Solgant arrow.

The keening stopped abruptly, and the quiet was worse than the song. Zorn's nerves were strung tighter than the great bowstring that strained like a live thing against his hands. No doubt the warriors below were already scrambling up, freed from Zorn's defense by the now-silent climber. He must not think of them; nor of Gurd; nor of Eloch, now also down with an arrow in him; nor of the dread curse reserved for traitors. *"He who turns his spear against his brother. . . "*

The blood cry again, shrill and close. And in the moment of its coming, the singer stood outlined bold and straight upon the cliff, his long spear upraised for throwing. In that moment, too, Zorn swung around, aiming his arrow at the singer's breast, and saw that it was Gryth.

Such a little thing, to let loose the arrow that strained

against his arm, demanding to be set free. "... *he who sheds his brother's blood* ..." Not Gryth. No matter the upraised spear. Not now or ever. Yet how the arrow fought him.

Even as he saw Gryth's shaft hurtling toward him, he lowered the heavy bow a little. For his arm was tired, achingly tired, and there was now no need.

Then the spear took him in the side, and the rebellious Solgant bow had leapt from his hands, and he was on his back, sick and half-dazed, against a slab of stone.

The stars seemed close, close enough to touch, almost, if only he had the strength. It was odd that they should shine so calm and undisturbed while here below the kill-keening was once again echoing through the rocks, passed along from one warrior to another. It held a triumphant note now that told of a traitor taken.

He did not know how long he had lain there, how long he might have till Gryth and Guroc and the others reached him. He had begun to hurt, his whole side molten fire that exploded anew with every breath he took. He was glad of the pain. It spoke of a death wound, saying that Gryth's spear had gone deep and true. How much better to die here on the mountain than to face King Myrgg and the Council, dishonored and forsworn—

Let him not think of that. Let him think of Llyndreth. He hoped she had held fast in her cave, as he had bade her. If she won free, it had not all been for nothing.

At the thought of Llyndreth, he came aware of the arm ring biting into his flesh where he lay upon it. They would not let him keep it. Guroc, before all others, would take it from him.

It was Llyndreth's one gift, all the thanks he had ever got for his troubles, and to think of Guroc gloating over it was more than he could bear. If Gryth might have it .. but then Gryth would no longer want anything of his. Or if he but had a way to send it back to Llyndreth . . .

He would see, at any rate, that Guroc did not get it. He turned himself, shutting his teeth against the waves of pain that set his head spinning, and managed somehow to get his arm free. Then he must twist himself even more to get the other arm across his body, must summon up the strength to fumble at the catch.

It was a strong, solid clasp, that. Perhaps a Danturin had worked it after all. And Dantur's Bones, but his fingers were clumsy . . .

Long before the clasp gave, he knew all too well what a ruin his side was. He had to pause more than once and press his hand to the pain and then begin again to struggle feebly with the arm ring.

It fell free at last. One thing more, and then he could rest. He grasped the metal band and, with what little strength he had, sent it skittering along the rocks.

It had not gone far, he knew. He was too weak for that. But if the warriors were busy with him and did not look closely . . . if the Solgants chanced by luck to come searching for him in this place . . . if the sun caught the glint of bare metal . . .

Too many ifs by far. Yet Guroc, at least, would not wear it. And the thing might somehow come to pass.

He was very tired. His thoughts were as sluggish as his arm had been, and his side throbbed wickedly. Even the pale stars seemed cruelly bright. Let her know what I meant if the arm ring reaches her, he thought wearily. Let her know that I sent it in leave-taking.

He fixed his gaze upon the calm, cruel stars.

The stars vanished. Gryth's face, filled with loathing, had blotted them out. Zorn shut his eyes against the sight.

He could not so easily shut out the flat, emotionless voice. "Sa," Gryth said. "Guroc was right, and I have played the fool. Even when you broke faith with me, I tried to shield you. And now you have borne arms against the Danturi."

There was so much Zorn longed to tell him—and nothing whatever that Gryth would understand.

"Was it not enough," Gryth said, no longer trying to keep the bitterness from his voice, "that you must betray your own people? Must you needs misuse our hearth bond in the doing?"

Their hearth bond. Beside its loss, the wound in Zorn's side was a small, poor pain. But he was tired, too tired to form the thought into words. Nor would Gryth believe him if he tried to speak.

"You should have died from my spear," said Gryth. "Let you know my heart was light when I threw it."

Could Gryth truly mean that, even now? Zorn opened his

eyes, hoping to find some trace of relenting. Instead, he saw Guroc beyond Gryth's shoulder.

"I hoped you were dead," Gryth went on, "for now I shall share in your dishonor. When the people make a mock of you, saying 'Spit on Zorn the traitor,' they will say more behind their hands.

" 'He was hearth friend to the king's heir,' they will say. 'For long, they were spear brothers together.'

"But I will give them yet another thing to talk of. Let them tell how I was first to pay the traitor's due." With that, Gryth spat full in Zorn's face and walked away.

Zorn lay blinking, too weak even to wipe away the spittle or to care that Guroc was kneeling beside him.

"It was a fine throwing spear that Gryth carried," Guroc remarked. "I do remember that his hearth friend, a great captain of warriors, helped him to perfect the balance. But Gryth will not want it longer. A spear tainted with traitor's blood is no true weapon."

Hot waves of pain swept through Zorn as Guroc wrenched the spear from his side. Dimly, from inside his swift-spinning world, he heard the sound of splintering wood. Then peaceful darkness took him.

OF ALL THE WEARY, DISHEARTENED HORSEMEN, LORD ROTHWYN
sagged heaviest in his saddle. His was the blame. An evil,
wicked bird it was that had filled his ear with glory songs
and sent him warring against the goblins. What a fool he had
been to listen!

It was not the loss of glory he minded so much. Nor the
fiery spear gash along his arm. He had lost so much more
than battles. There was his father's manor burned to the
ground. And gone with it all the strength and peace his father
had worked for.

There were the good men who had followed him, now
dead. Whatever would he tell their women when he returned?

If he returned. If the goblins let him.

And there was his sister.

Like a fool, he had thought the Danturi weak because they
did not attack. Like a fool, he had split his forces. Last night
the goblins had all but slaughtered his raiding party. He dared
not hope the main camp had fared better.

Desperately, Rothwyn scrubbed at his forehead as if he could dash his fears away along with the sweat. He must think now as a commander. He must think of the men who remained, not of his sister only.

Yet his mind kept wandering to Llyndreth. What a bother she had seemed when he was a boy. She'd been trying always to be a man-child and older than she really was. Once she had taken, without his knowing it, the new bow their father had given him and had lost three of its fine arrows forever. Afterward, at his insistence, their father had whipped her, as he seldom ever did. Llydreth had wanted to cry; but, stubbornly, she would not. The look in her eyes had made him sorry for his tale-telling long before the punishment was over.

She had not cried, either, the day he rode to war. She had smiled all the while, till the last sight he had of her, a stiff, desperate little smile that seemed ever in danger of crumbling.

She would not have cried last night—

Without really feeling the pain of it, Rothwyn hugged the cloth-bound arm closer to his side. If he had not come to these cursed mountains . . .

It was not he who saw the odd-looking figure on the hillside. "My lord—" The archer who rode beside him had already seized an arrow from his quiver. "Look yonder, my lord," he said quietly, fitting the arrow to his bow.

The figure—really head and shoulders only, and those muffled in a great, hooded cloak that revealed nothing—

poked timidly out from a hole in the cliff wall. A small hole that one would not otherwise have noticed.

"Aim your arrow," said Rothwyn, "but do not let fly until I command."

Whatever it was threw up its hands to shield its eyes against the glare. It was then that the cloak fell back, showing the bright hair beneath, hair that was like Rothwyn's own sun gold thatch.

Lowering his bow, the archer gave a great, wordless shout. But already Lord Rothwyn had thrown himself off his horse and was running up the slope, stumbling over loose rocks but scarcely pausing, hurrying to clasp his sister in his arms.

She did cry this time, from joy and relief, and she was not alone in her tears. Before what men he had left, Rothwyn Goldbeard, warlord among the Solgants, wept openly. And there was not one in sight of it who scorned him.

Llyndreth blinked owlishly and hid her face once more in Rothwyn's shoulder. "It is so good to see the sun again, yet it makes my eyes ache terribly." Her brother felt her stiffen.

"What is it?"

"The sunlight. I know now how it feels to a Danturin." She looked up anxiously despite the glare. "Have you seen Zorn?"

"Your renegade goblin? I have seen too many of his brethren this night. Perhaps he was with them. They all look as alike as hen eggs in a nest."

"Do they so?" Llyndreth stood as straight as a young warlord, and her eyes were very angry. "And yet his brethren would not have risked their lives to keep me safe in yonder cave. They would not have gone out alone to lead the Shadow Warriors on a false trail."

"More like," muttered one of the men who had come close to listen, "more like he joined his brethren."

Llyndreth stamped her foot. "He did not!" But instantly the anger faded from her voice, leaving only the fear. "Oh, Rothwyn, we must help him! He would have come back if he could. He took Etheryll to hide her so that she would not lead them to me, and he did not come back. He is surely hurt or—or—"

"He must look elsewhere for his help," said Rothwyn slowly. "His spear brothers have seen to it that we can barely help ourselves."

For the first time Llyndreth really looked at the men around her. They were a pitiful few, ragged and bloody, scarce one unwounded. Their mounts stood sweat-flecked and drooping.

"Yes," said Rothwyn, "the goblins have beaten us, and soundly. I had thought they would finish us all, and it is a thing beyond understanding that they did not. We were at the end of our strength, caught fast. And then, toward morning, when all things looked hopeless, they set up that awful howling of theirs. After they had yelled awhile, as only goblins can, they simply disappeared. I cannot think what led them from the kill.

"But we are at their mercy now. The one thing left for us is to get as far away as possible before nightfall."

"But first you will look for Zorn."

Rothwyn looked down at her uncomfortably. "Little sister," he said, "believe me. By all that I hold dear, I would if I could. But I must see to the survivors in our camp, if there be any. And I've a duty to these men who ride beside me. I cannot risk their lives for one—"

Llyndreth finished for him. Scornfully. "For one goblin.

"Go then, Rothwyn. Look to your men. I will hunt for Zorn. It is my debt, after all."

"Do not talk like a fool. You know you must go with us. It is death to stay here."

"Then mayhap I shall choose death."

Rothwyn exploded. "Lord of the Sun, Llyndreth, will you never grow up? You are willful and obstinate always. Was it so you might die, think you, that your goblin hid you in the cave? Did he risk his life for that?"

Llyndreth's face tightened. The freckles seemed to stand out more plainly around her nose. She looked past her brother, past the knot of wearied, battered men. "There is a pattern to it," she said finally. "I must be the most useless creature ever born. It was Helgydd told me first. 'Let you flee,' she said. 'You can do nothing to save the castle.'

"Angborn next. I was sure to prove a hindrance in your war camp and should turn back instead.

"Even Zorn said the same. I should be useless when the camp was attacked, so for your sake I should save myself. Now, for his sake, I should run away.

"Well, I own the truth. All of you were right. I have helped no one. Yet this one time more, I must be willful.

"Rothwyn." Her eyes met his steadily. "He is my friend.

Shall I live out my life knowing I left my friend helpless and alone? How if you left Eathrydd so?"

It was not the same, thought Rothwyn. Eathrydd was his own kind, had been his friend since they both of them could scarcely toddle. By blood right, this Zorn was enemy to Llyndreth.

Yet he could see that Llyndreth marked no difference. For her, it was exactly the same.

"We will search," he said gruffly. "I will send out all the men I can spare. But for one hour only. I am a fool to risk so much.

"At one hour's end, we will go, no matter what, and you with us."

His sister's eyes thanked him.

It was the horse master who brought word. Silently, he beckoned Rothwyn away from Llyndreth. "My lord," he said, when Rothwyn had drawn close, "we did not find the Danturin. But we found my lady's pony. And we found this. It was yours once, I think." He handed over the shattered remains of Rothwyn's second-best bow.

"He was none so bad a fellow for a goblin," said the man, with grudging admiration. "Used to come around my horse pens a lot, he did, since the men would have nothing to do with him. My horses came not to fear the goblin smell of him. And of course they never minded his ugly looks. Some of them would go right up to be petted.

"And he was a fighter. You can say that, sure. The men used to call him a coward and a turncoat, and they were right enough, I guess, as to turncoat. But he was no coward, Father of Light, he was not. And no spy, neither, as some folks thought. He'd have made a good Solgant, I guess, if the men had not misliked—"

"Never mind that," said Rothwyn shortly. "What did you find?"

"Well, he had made his stand on a kind of shelf with the cliff at his back so they couldn't come at him easy and rocks at the front to shield him. And that was where we found the bow, you see, and one of the arrows with it. Never got to use that last, I guess, poor fellow.

"The rest were below, and he had used them as pretty as any Solgant archer, only there was but one of him and not so many arrows, either, as he might've wished for. And you know, Lord Rothwyn, sir, there was as many goblins on this cursed mountain last night as there are rocks today. There was just one end to look for."

"But you did not find his body?"

"No, my lord Rothwyn." The horse master glanced uneasily in Llyndreth's direction. "We found blood, though. She will take it hard, I guess, the lady Llyndreth will. But we did find blood. There was a Danturin spear, broken in two, with blood well up the shaft of it. And blood on the rocks, too, a whole pool of it, dried hard. And on another thing, too. Let you come with me, sir, and I'll show you."

He took an object from his saddle pocket. "Don't this be the lady Llyndreth's arm ring? She gave it to him, I guess. I fastened it up in case she was watching, so I'd not come riding up waving it under her nose and it all bloody like a flag flying to say the Danturin was killed." He put the arm ring into Rothwyn's hands. "I don't envy you, sir, if you don't mind my saying it, the tale you'll have to tell her."

He mounted and looked down at Rothwyn. "It's a pity, I guess, that he wasn't born a Solgant. I'll not shed tears over a goblin's dying. Not me. They killed my grandsire down at the sheep pens, they did, during a raid. But he did handle himself pretty and warriorlike during a fight. And my horses liked him, and the lady Llyndreth. . . ."

Rothwyn did not answer. He was looking down at the blood-caked arm ring in his hands.

Three blasts on the war horn. Three blasts to bring back the searchers. Llyndreth came to Rothwyn in a rush. "What does it mean, the horn? Does it mean they've found Zorn?"

"It means we are leaving. Get you ready, Llyndreth."

"But it has not been an hour. You know it has been no hour!"

There was no way to make it kind news, no time, even, to give her for grieving. Perhaps bluntness was best. "Thorvald Horse Master brought word just now. They have found where your Danturin fell. A Shadow Warrior's spear found him." It sounded harsher, even, than he had expected. "I am sorry, little sister," he said more gently.

She did not make any sound, but it was enough to make you weep, watching the hope in her face die. It was a true word the horse master had spoken: "I do not envy you the telling her."

"Did they bring him back?" she asked finally. "Or did they

heap stones above him. He would not mind the stones and darkness. The Danturi are born to them."

It would be easier if he lied to her. Easier for them both. But he had never lied to his sister. "They did not find his body. The Danturi must have taken it."

"Then he might not be dead! He might be wounded only. They cannot be sure." A new alarm struck her. "They held him traitor. If they took him alive and helpless—"

"Never torture yourself with that. My men were very sure."

"How should they be sure? How, and his body not there to tell them?"

It was like his sister to press him. It made him angrier that he must hurt her further. "The blood told them, Llyndreth. There was overmuch blood and a spear that had gone very deep."

"Men have bled before and still lived."

Stubborn! Lord of Light, but she was stubborn! Next she would be demanding that they attack the Danturi on the faint half hope that Zorn was living. Rothwyn had meant to cleanse the arm ring before he let her see it. But he would be cruel if he must. Since it taught her nothing to be told of blood, he would let her look on it.

"See, sister, and understand. Your Danturin died of a spear thrust, and he knew well that he was dying." Rothwyn brought the arm ring from beneath his cloak. "He sent back your gift in leave-taking."

She shrank back, her eyes wide with horror at the sight of the stains. "Take it away. It is blood-cursed. Angborn said it was a thing of power, and I wanted to give Zorn a good gift. But what good gift brings death with it?" She paused, then went on in an odd, harsh voice. "Perhaps it was evil-powered, after all. And I gave it to him—"

"Llyndreth!" said Rothwyn sharply. "Try not to be foolish. It was not you who killed the fellow, nor yet an arm ring. It was the sharp point of a Danturin spear. That, only."

"Oh, I threw no spear. Yet I was his doom-bringer, still. Since first I came to the mountain and put him in my debt, he could look for no better ending." Lyndreth's face twisted. "Do as you will with the arm ring so that I need not see it."

A memory stirred in Rothwyn, though it was long before he caught the whole of it. It was the look in his sister's eyes that he remembered. Just so had his father's looked, old and dismal and empty, on the day he buried their mother.

17

ROTHWYN'S HEART WAS LIGHTER NOW THAT THEY HAD LEFT THE mountain behind them. Ever during their hurried flight had he expected to hear the wild war song of the Danturi and to find his exhausted, half-crippled party pinned to earth by a swarm of singing spears.

Once, indeed, spears had come flying from nowhere, and two men had fallen wounded. But it was no such deadly attack as he had dreaded, for no goblins had come surging out of invisible rock lairs to surround and destroy them. They had met Danturin scouts only, he supposed, or a pair of hunters caught almost as unprepared as he.

Ahead, now, he could see the wild, twisted forest growth that stood sentinel around Angborn's domain. For all its forbidding look, Rothwyn rejoiced to see it. It was not home, to be sure. And the Eodan—well, you could not be quite sure of someone who changed size at will. But giant or no giant, whatever strange powers the fellow might possess, he had stood friend to Llyndreth. And she seemed to think him wise.

They had need of wisdom. Rothwyn stole a quick glance at his sister. Her face was still, too still for his liking. He did not think she had wept once since he told her how Zorn had fallen, and he was very sure she had not smiled.

There was calm, thought Rothwyn, and then there was calm. The one kind came from mastering yourself when it was needful. The other—and his mind misgave him that this was Llyndreth's case—came when something inside you died or drew down, at least, so far inside the darkness of yourself that it seemed past finding.

With luck, he told himself hopefully, the Eodan might have some lore that would unlock the darkness.

"Look yonder," he said, pointing at the forest. "Do you think your giant friend knows we are coming?"

"Perhaps."

But the prospect brought no light to his sister's eyes, and it was assuredly no spur that hurried her along, for she reined Etheryll around and brought the pony to a halt.

"What are you doing?" demanded Rothwyn in alarm.

"I am looking back. I shall come along presently."

Why, in the name of Light, should she want to look at those miserable mountains again? For his part, he would put them behind him gladly. He would forget, if he could, the trap he'd blundered into and the horrors of his ruined camp. Could not Llyndreth also try to forget?

"It grows late," Rothwyn said, trying without success to hide his annoyance. He was tired, bone-tired, and his spear-gashed arm hurt.

"Ride on, then. I have told you that I will follow."

Her voice shut him out, as it did in all things now. Reluctantly, Rothwyn obeyed.

Something was thundering toward Rothwyn through the brush, and his horse, tired though it was, rose to its hind legs in fear. "Hold steady," Rothwyn murmured reassuringly, remembering what his sister had told him of her visit to the Eodan's forest. "It is only Angborn's great stag. Naught to fear, old warrior. Naught at all."

But his hands were damper than they had been. It was one thing to tell yourself to be easy, another to do it with an unseen something hurtling toward you, the size of a small mountain by the sound of it, and at full speed, too.

It would be well, Rothwyn thought, If the Eodan would teach his messenger a little courtesy in greeting strangers—

And then the stag was upon him, swerving past, barely missing him, just as Llyndreth had recalled it, digging its hooves into the ground for a sudden stop.

With dismay, Rothwyn discovered that he had been holding a great, indrawn breath. He let it out slowly and settled himself in the saddle, straight enough for dignity but loose enough to show that he had not been afraid.

"Llyndreth's brother, I suppose," said the stag in the purest of Solgant accents.

Rothwyn's mouth was hanging open. He took pains to shut it.

The stag pawed the ground impatiently. It gazed at Rothwyn, its huge brown eyes sharper and more penetrating, he thought, than even a magical animal's should be. It was as if the cursed deer were probing his mind, seeing, mistake after mistake, all the miswrought plans that had ended lately in disaster. Rothwyn's eyes fell.

Almost immediately, he raised them. It was an ill day when a Solgant lord could not meet a stag's eyes.

But within that instant, the stag's great rack of antlers had begun dissolving into swirls of smoke. Or mist. Or fog. Whatever the substance, it wrapped itself, shifting yet impenetrable, around the animal.

The sun lord sat, clutching his saddle horn. Presently, the mist dissolved, and he was facing no stag but a tall, brown, weather-beaten man, whose clothes fit him loosely as though they had been cut for someone even larger.

"Have you lost your voice, Lord Rothwyn?" asked the man. "Must I take speech with your horse instead?

"I could, you know," he added dryly. "And get more sense out of him, too, perhaps."

With difficulty, Rothwyn collected himself. "My sister had said that you could change size but not shape," he said in as dignified a voice as he could muster. "I had not thought to see you as a stag."

What might have been a smile crossed the old-young face briefly. "It may be that I did not tell her precisely the whole truth. I have the shaping of those animals I know best. I can do a stag if I like. Or a hare. Or"—he made a wry face—"a sheep, if I could stand the boredom.

"Once, very long ago, much longer than you could possibly imagine, I took the form of a swallow. However, I did not care for flying. It gave me a light, hollow feeling, most disconcerting to one as large as I habitually am, and I could never entirely get the trick of balance. I was dizzy the whole time and a little sick at my stomach, too. I have never been gladder of anything than to get the feel of solid ground beneath my feet again.

"I thought afterward that while flying would no doubt be a great convenience, I could turn stag and run quite fast enough for most purposes. And as for being able to see great distances so that you know all that is going on about you, I was too dizzy and frightened to see much of anything. My bird friends can tell me anything I need to know, which serves as well as if I went flapping about the skies myself and felt miserably sick afterward."

He shook his head. "No, Eodans were not meant for flying, no more than Solgants are suited for burrowing into mountains—" He broke off abruptly. "Where is your sister?"

"Just behind us. At the edge of your forest. She was bent on staying there alone for a little." Rothwyn forgot the shock of the Eodan's transformation, forgot even the less-than-impressive figure he must have cut watching it. "Fortune grant that you can help her," he said anxiously.

"Help her?" Angborn frowned. "She is back safely. What need of help has she now?"

Where to begin? "Well," said Rothwyn uncertainly, "you remember the Danturin she found—"

"Her goblin? Assuredly." Angborn's frown grew. "If he did aught to harm her—"

"No. Oh, no." It was a good thing, after all, Rothwyn thought, that Llyndreth had lagged behind. If she'd heard the Eodan say that—"It was the other way. The harm fell on him."

It was a hard thing to tell, somehow. Perhaps the guilt his sister felt was catching. "He saved her, more than once. The other goblins—his fellow warriors, I mean—they cast him out." The arm ring in his saddle pocket lay solid against his leg. He was aware of it, suddenly, remembering the stains he had scrubbed away. Almost, it seemed to burn his thigh. "They killed him for it."

He had not supposed anything could disturb the Eodan's massive calm, no more than you could disturb a rock or an ancient tree trunk; but Angborn looked startled. No. More than startled. Shaken.

"I had not thought it possible," Angborn said slowly, "that a Danturin should give his life for a Solgant. It was strange enough when your sister . . . but then she had not so great a reason for hatred as the Danturi. . . . No, I should have thought to see the mountain crumbled into dust before such a thing came about." He sighed. "It is as well they killed him. Else how they should have made him suffer! But it will be a sore burden to your sister."

"A burden! She thinks of nothing else. I know I should be grateful to the Danturin for saving her life. And yet"—Rothwyn knotted his fists helplessly—"yet she had as well be dead as like this. If she is to spend her life grieving for a—" He stopped, flushing.   ,

"For a goblin?" There was sadness in the Eodan's smile. "The old hatreds pinch hard still!"

"Yes! For a goblin. It is so that our people will think of him, and she belongs to our people. If you have the power, help her to forget!"

"Gently, Sun Lord!" Angborn grimaced. "Was there ever such a people as the Solgants for impatience? Grief is no swift-racing steed, that you can put spurs to it and hurry it along. I will help your sister—but in my own way, as I think best.

"While I go to her, let your party follow my path." Already the thick forest was closing around Rothwyn's men. For a moment Angborn's eyes danced with mischief. "It will not lose you. Never yet has it lost a guest against my bidding."

The sun was sliding into darkness. But not willingly, nor in peace. As a last act of defiance, it set Goblin Mountain aflame. Once before, when she had barely set out on her journey, Llyndreth had seen those dark rocks so: forbidding clefts, shadows bathed in blood. She had trembled at the sight.

She knew now how terrible the mountain really was. But she knew much more also. And she could not talk of those things to Rothwyn.

Could she speak of them to Marnne, she wondered. Could she make her best of friends picture the delicate lacework of stone in the cavern of fire? And what of Zorn's hand, strong and gentle in the darkness—? The reluctant brush of his fingers against her hair in parting—? Dared she hope that Marnne would even listen?

She did not know that Angborn had come until he spoke. "So the Danturin is dead," he said, "and no one will understand."

It was as though he had seen into her heart. But he, too, she remembered, had despised goblins.

"He had a name. Let you use it."

"So he did," said the Eodan. "And though his people will spit on its memory, I will do it honor. He was Zorn, Captain of Shadow Warriors, the first of his kind since first they took refuge in the mountain to break the bonds of hatred."

She had wept in Angborn's arms then, with long-held tears that had refused to come before. "Rothwyn thinks," she said afterward, when she had dried her eyes and spoken of her troubles, "that I am sorrowing for Zorn's death. But that is only a little part of it. He was a warrior and not afraid to die.

"I grieve more for what happened in our camp. Zorn was alone there, shamed before my people and his own. While I —who should have seen how unhappy he was—I had my brother again and my own kind around me and was blind to his loneliness.

"And at the last, when he was hurt and helpless—even then, he had no friend beside him."

"So now," said Angborn quietly, "it is you who will be alone."

"Alone? Not I. I have my people still."

"Perhaps. But you have left something of yourself on the mountain and brought back part of Zorn in its place. Never again can you be all Solgant.

"How will it be when those you hold dearest speak of goblin treachery and you remember ... things you should not? Will you not feel a stranger in your own halls?" He shook his head. "Already the lord Rothwyn has asked that I help you forget. But I will not. It is not fitting that love should die so soon."

"Love?" Llyndreth looked up, startled.

The Eodan smiled slightly. "What name else would you call it, Sun's Daughter? I have lived a long while and have seen many men die for what they called honor. But to give up honor itself, that takes love. And what else can make one ache for another's hurts as you are doing this moment?

"I am glad now that I gave you the arm ring. I was not sure that a Solgant should have it. But now—" His glance fell on her bare arm, and he frowned. "Surely, you have not lost it! I warned you it might be a thing of power."

"I did not lose it," Llyndreth said with a hint of defiance. "I gave it to Zorn. I had cost him so much, and it was all I had to give."

"I cannot say you did wrong. It was a gift worth the giving, and he had earned it." The Eodan paused, considering. "Another Danturin has it now, I suppose. That is entirely too bad. Who can tell what its new owner is like or what will come of it if the thing has power?"

"No. My brother has it. His horse master found it among the rocks. Take it back, Angborn. Please." Llyndreth's voice trembled. "I cannot wear it again. It had—it has blood on it."

The Eodan sighed in relief. "It is safe, at least. But how came it to be in the rocks?"

"I suppose Zorn lost it. When he . . ." She faltered. "He fought hard, the horse master said."

"So it fell off in battle, think you?" Angborn snorted. "Not that arm ring. It had a strong, good clasp. It never came loose in fighting. Someone undid the catch. And I scarcely think it was the Danturi. They would not have cast away such a well-wrought arm ring.

"And if not the Danturi, there was only Zorn.

"Tell me, Sun's Daughter, why Zorn himself would have unclasped the armlet."

"I—I do not know."

"Do you not? It is in my mind that you are afraid to know. And also"—Angborn's voice was stern—"that it is somewhat overlate for you to play the coward.

"It was not my arm Zorn meant to wear the ring. It is yours more than ever now, yours by double giving. I think you cannot choose but keep the gift.

"Think on this when you wear it," he added more gently. "He did not die alone."

"What can you mean? You know he was alone!"

"Not so, Sun's Daughter. If there was giving in his heart, he was not alone. When one gives, one is never alone."

* * *

Rothwyn glared at the Eodan's hearth fire. "Wisdom!" he spat out the word. "She said that you had wisdom, and I felt sure that you would cheer her up. And what have you done instead? Talked her into wearing that accursed arm ring, that's what, so she'll brood more than ever about the Danturin.

"She'll come back all smiles, I suppose," he added sarcastically, "after going without her dinner to wander away by herself in the pitch-black dark. I don't see what good it's done you, living since Goblin Mountain was scarce more than a molehill, if that's your idea of wisdom!"

Angborn puffed at his pipe with hard-held patience. "I have told you. Grief is a steed that must travel its own pace. There's no spurring it on or holding it back. Your sister will be no better for it if you try."

Rothwyn grunted. "She's been gone a while and a while. Does she plan to wander among your trees all night? We've had a long, hard journey, and it's time she was abed."

Yawning, he fingered the fresh bandage on his arm. "Time all of us were. It's a funny kind of wisdom that keeps her from food and sleep—"

"Patience—" began the Eodan. He broke off suddenly and sprang to his feet at the sound of a cry from the darkness.

Not a loud cry, but one to raise the hairs along a man's neck, be he Eodan or Solgant. A cry of pain, mayhap, and fear, yet there seemed something of joy in it also.

"Llyndreth!" Rothwyn shouted. Then he was running, Angborn beside him, toward the darkness and the trees and the terror of that cry.

She leaned limply against a tree trunk. Her face shone pale in the moonlight, and the arm ring dangled, unclasped, from her right hand.

When her brother seized the other, it seemed very cold to the touch. "Are you hurt?" he demanded. "What is it? What frightened you?"

Llyndreth did not answer at once. Pulling free of him, she linked the armlet together and held it cupped in her hands.

"I saw him," she whispered, studying the circlet of metal as though she had not seen it before.

"Saw whom?" snapped Rothwyn. But he knew already who it was she meant.

"Zorn. He is not dead. But Lord of Light—" Her face twisted at some memory.

"Nonsense! You're tired out, and you dozed, that's all. You've been brooding too much about the fellow, and"— Rothwyn looked accusingly at the Eodan—"this arm ring business was too much for you."

"It was no dream," said Llyndreth quietly. "It was the arm ring, yes. But no dream."

"Come to bed, sister. Tomorrow you'll feel foolish for putting such stock in nightmares."

"I'll not feel foolish! It was not at all like dreaming. I saw Zorn. And then I was Zorn. Was inside him or a part of him or—

"Oh!" she burst out, her eyes filling with tears, "it was real, it *was*! But how can I possibly explain it so it makes sense?"

The Eodan touched her arm. "Come sit at my hearth-place,

Llyndreth. With a good cup of honey mead to warm you, it may be that the telling will come easier."

Llyndreth set down the cup Angborn had given her and knotted her hands together. "It is a thing of power," she said, her eyes on the arm ring that lay so innocent-looking on the table before her. "I knew there was magic about it, but not like this. Nothing at all like this."

She turned to her brother. "I *was* thinking of Zorn," she said, "wishing that I could undo all my mistakes. But I did not dream. I put on the arm ring, and then I saw him.

"He was lying. . . ." She faltered. "Lying, all limp and ragged, in a cave. But he looked unlike himself, somehow, though I knew him at once." Llyndreth looked up in puzzlement. "If I could only remember—

"Why, he was bare-faced," she exclaimed in surprise. "As if someone had scraped away the fur and done rather a bad job of it at that."

"I would never have dreamed that," she told Rothwyn with a triumphant glance. "Never!" The triumph faded as a new thought struck her. "It was so he would look more like —more like us, wasn't it? To show that he was no longer a Danturin."

She bit her lip. "Do you remember when first we found him, Angborn? 'I am Zorn, Captain of Shadow Warriors,' he said, as though that meant king of the world.

"And now . . . the arm ring showed me other Danturi taunting him, calling him traitor. And he tried—tried to stand against them—and could not.

"Afterward, there came a time when I saw nothing more. It was all feeling. I was a part of Zorn, feeling what he felt. There was pain all through me. And shame. And loneliness. But the worst was knowing that things would never, never be any better. Knowing that, I wanted to die.

"Before long," she said, shuddering, "it was past bearing, and I—I pulled off the arm ring."

"And a good job that was!" put in Rothwyn. "It is an ill-omened thing that gives you false visions. Let me have the thing once more, and I'll destroy it. Whatever it takes. If burying won't do, I'll melt it."

"No!" Llyndreth clasped her hands protectively around the arm-ring. She looked at Angborn. "It was no dream?" The faintest hint of a question in her voice hardened at once into certainty. "It was like your shape changing, I think. Only it was not shape I changed but spirit. What manner of arm ring is it that can do so much?"

The Eodan shook his head doubtfully. "Let you be careful, Llyndreth. You must take care with a thing of power."

But Llyndreth was no longer listening. "Past bearing," she whispered. "After such a little while, it was past bearing. And for me, it was but an arm ring's vision. If it were real . . ." She buried her head in her arms. "If it were real and endless, how could one endure?"

WITH DAYBREAK CAME THUNDER. AND THE THUNDERER WAS LORD
Rothwyn. "Eodan!" he stormed. "Is this not the king of evil
chances! And it's your fault. Never say it is not. Lord of
Light, but I hold you accountable!"

Angborn opened one brown eye. "What's amiss, Solgant?"

"What's amiss? Llyndreth's gone; that's what's amiss! Oh,
you take it very calmly, you do. She's turned back to that
mountain—you know it as well as I do—and as smooth as
merryday pudding you ask me what's amiss!"

Rothwyn ground his teeth. "What would our father say to
me? Yes, and our lady mother?"

"It is no more," said Angborn quietly, "than I expected."

"You expected! So did I expect. And since I could not bind
my sister hand and foot, I set guards to watch her. Yet she's
gone, and they saw nothing." Rothwyn threatened to explode
again. "It is you I hold to blame. You and that cursed arm
ring!"

The Eodan made no reply. "What will you do?" he asked instead.

"What choice have I? I shall go after her, naturally, and bring her back. I can't let her go rushing into danger because of some idiotic dream."

"And if it was no dream?"

"Of course it was."

"Yet I know beyond all question," said Angborn, "that she did not dream."

Rothwyn stared. "Beyond all question? How?"

"Because the armlet has done much the same for me."

"You said—" Rothwyn sputtered angrily. "You said you knew nothing of its powers."

"I said I knew but little of the whole. And that was true enough. Listen, Solgant, and I will tell you what knowledge I do have.

"I said to your sister that I was the last of all my kind. But yet I was not always alone. I can remember the time when I had father and mother and grandsire. And cousins also. But let my cousins go, for they are nothing to the point.

"I was yet a child then, but I roamed far and wide in my play and was gone for long and long as you Solgants count time. Your days were as nothing to the Eodans, and as for danger, no harm had ever threatened us in those days. We had been kings over this part of the world since the beginning of memory, and among us, my grandsire was highest. The Danturi had come long since, but the Danturi were a little people and free-moving hunters. We scarcely recked of the Danturi, no more than you fret in your castle, Lord Rothwyn, over squirrels that dance from tree to tree. Not until your people came.

"Then it was that your forefathers began to push the Danturi onto the mountain. And yet you did not trouble us either. We did not guess our days were numbered.

"So I roamed the hills and forests, playing alone. It was always so, for I was the youngest, by far, of all our people. And on a day, I came home as always after such a roaming.

"Yet not as always. This day I came home to quarreling.

" 'We are the Eodans, mind-bound to all,' someone cried out. 'What need had one of us for such a frail Danturin charm?'

" 'Not so frail, perhaps,' my father muttered, 'if it was wrought by Dantur himself. His power linked to ours might yield a strength that all must bend to. He held uncommon knowledge for his kind.'

" 'We stand no friend to Solgants or to traitors,' called another. 'But hereafter Dantur's people will hold us foe!'

" 'Syngarion alone should suffer for it!' voices clamored. 'His was the misdeed.'

"Then my grandsire Eldeon roared fiercely. 'Shame to one, shame to all!' he thundered. 'Let one of us deal in treachery, we are all besmirched. Shall the Danturi go homeless and the Eodans lose their claim to honor?'

"Never had I seen my grandsire angry, and I clutched at my father's arm. Yet he, too, spoke to me sharply. 'Bide still, Angborn,' he snapped. 'This is no matter for younglings!'

"So I fled the fury in their eyes and voices. I wandered

farther than ever I had done. And when, at last, I returned ..."
The Eodan drew a long, deep breath. "I came back to nothing, Solgant. My mother, father, all were gone without a trace."

He fell silent, drawing back, it seemed, to that faraway time.

"And what did you then," Rothwyn prompted after a little, "alone and only a child?"

"Why, searched, of course. And called to the four winds without an answer. Also," Angborn added quite matter-of-factly, "I wept whole rivers. I had not known what it was to be afraid before, you see. Or lonely. It's different being alone when you know there's nothing to return to.

"Before long, I went to the mountain. It was special to the Eodans before ever the Danturi set foot there. But ..." An old anger stirred in Angborn's voice. "The Danturi drove me away. Their king stood amid his Shadow Warriors, who bristled with their sharpened spears. 'Let you be gone, youngling,' he said. 'The time of the Old Ones is past now. They have left the mountain to us.'"

"Why did you not go back when you were grown and take vengeance?" Rothwyn studied Angborn's great bulk admiringly. "You could kill a good many goblins, I think."

"It was long and long before I was grown, Solgant. That king and his son and his son's son beyond him, they were in their graves before I reached manhood. By then it no longer mattered so very much.

"But hush so I can tell you of the arm ring. I came here at last, for it was here that my mother and father had held their homesteading. And on a day I reached into the trunk of a great, stricken hollow tree where I was wont to keep my treasures. Then my fingers touched the cold metal, and I drew out the arm ring.

"Never had I seen it before, but I knew that it had been left for me within my secret place. So I clasped it on my arm—I was no bigger than a Solgant then, and it fit me much as it does your sister.

"And here is the wonder of it, Sun's Child. When once I wore the thing, my mother was with me. Not to see or touch or speak to, but with me nonetheless. It was, even as your sister said, as though we were one, I inside her or else her mind inside my own. We were calm and happy together, the one of us."

"So your people were not dead?"

Angborn shrugged. "What is death, think you? I know only that she was gone and yet with me."

Rothwyn looked unconvinced. "I believe you dreamed it. I believe you wished so hard to have her back that it seemed to be so. And it is the same with Llyndreth."

"Do you? Yet when my people vanished, I had not reached an age to learn spell making. All the little I know—the changing of shape and size—came afterward, from my mother by way of the arm ring."

"Then why did she not teach you everything?"

For the first time Angborn looked sad. "In time," he said, "—oh, a very long time in Solgant years but not such a great while in the life of an Eodan—I began to forget my mother. It is the way of all living things to forget. It grew hard reaching out to her, even with the arm ring. By then, too, I could take the shape of animals and go with them for company. And at the last, my wrist outgrew the arm ring. Afterward, there were only memories."

He shook off the sadness. "All of which was so long ago I can scarce remember. I only spoke of it so you would understand what thing your sister wears."

"You knew," Rothwyn accused, growing angry again. "And yet you gave it to her. Why did you, Eodan?"

"Because it is no common Solgant who befriends a goblin. Because I wondered much what your sister might do with magic. Besides, it was a good gift to me always. It never brought me evil."

"Let us hope," said Rothwyn bitterly, "that Llyndreth can say the same when she's a goblin captive. You'd have better destroyed the thing before you gave it to her."

Angborn gazed at him in wonder. "What small vision the Solgants have! Never looking at the whole but only the part, only the one small, pitiful piece of now their minds can focus on. You would indeed destroy the arm ring, wouldn't you, because it is leading your sister back to Zorn?"

"To her death, rather. Of course I would destroy it."

"Then I shall go back with you. If you are bent on such folly, you are sure to need my help."

"Such help as you gave Llyndreth? I do not want it."

The giant smiled. "So you say, Llyndreth's brother. So you say now. Let you but try to destroy a thing of power, you may find you long for any help at all."

* * *

They had pushed hard all the day. And yet by nightfall they had caught no sight of Llyndreth.

"We should have overtaken her," Rothwyn fretted. "The goblins could not ... surely they could not have caught her so soon."

"Patience," said the Eodan soothingly. "With daybreak we shall find her."

"If she's not underground by then. Captive in some goblin hole."

"We, too, shall be captives unless we find a hole of our own."

"You'd say that. It's not your sister. You weren't charged on your father's deathbed to keep her safe. You've forgotten what it's like to love your family."

Angborn stroked the pocket of his cloak where Old Spinner rode inside. "Like enough, that's true," he said quietly. "I've forgotten many things."

"There's some moon, at least," Rothwyn muttered. "There was no moon when they cut us to pieces.

"We're near there, I think," he added reluctantly. "Near to where so many of my men died. I hope their spirits lie quietly. Their ghosts would be glad of a chance at me, I suppose. At the fool that led them into slaughter—"

He pulled his horses up suddenly. "Did you see that up there?"

"Up where?"

"Above us. To the right a little. A moving light. There— did you see it this time?" Rothwyn shifted uneasily in his saddle. "A pale light, not like any torch I know of—"

"No torch," agreed the Eodan. "It would have nothing to do with the Danturi at any rate. They need no lights."

"I have heard of ghost lights—" Suddenly Rothwyn swore in disgust. "What a warrior I am! To be fearing ghost lights when my sister—" He put spurs to his horse and rode on.

Up ahead the light shone and disappeared, then shone again briefly. An odd-colored, eerie light that could not be depended on to shine at all. Presently they saw it no more. The moon had hidden behind the clouds so that it was very dark.

And then another light sprang up, much closer this time. This was no ghost light certainly. It was a red gold flame that clung close to the ground and stayed in one place, properly, as fire should do.

"That's a cheery sight, Eodan," said Rothwyn with relief in his voice. "I think no ghost would warm itself at such a flame."

"Nor would a goblin. But they will not think it cheery. They mislike alien fires upon their mountain."

They moved ever closer, came at last to the circle of the fire. Llyndreth sat on a stone, light and shadows dancing across her face.

"I give you good evening, brother," she said. "And a farewell with the greeting. You had as lief turn your horse about now, for I am not going back, whatever you may think. You have come a long way this day for nothing."

Rothwyn sat his horse, sputtering. The right words would not come, however hard he tried. At last he dismounted, strode to the fire, and began kicking dirt into it. "What are you thinking of," he got out finally, "to build up such a flame? The goblins are bound to see it."

"So they will. It is why I built the fire."

Speechless, Rothwyn glared at her.

"It is this way," said Llyndreth cheerfully. "If I'm to help Zorn, I must speak with the Danturin king. And I could look a long while without finding him. So I should like to be taken instead. If I let the Danturi capture me—"

"And how," her brother interrupted, "if they do not wait to take you prisoner but simply make a pincushion of you with their spears?"

"Well ..." A small frown pinched Llyndreth's brows together. "I suppose there's some danger of that."

"*Some* danger!"

"Perhaps the arm ring would help me." The girl turned eagerly to the Eodan. "Did you see my light, Angborn? I've learned to make it glow of itself. As it did in the cave."

"In the cave? What cave?"

"Didn't I tell you? No, I suppose I didn't. I was not thinking ..." Her chin quivered, then stiffened. "I was not thinking of the cave when next I saw you.

"Well, I shall tell you now. It was when Zorn was hiding me. He took me to a cave, and there was a door within it, a great stone slab of a door leading to still another cave. And the arm ring began to glow when we came near the slab, and almost of itself the door opened for it—"

Angborn was on one knee beside her, his face tense. "What was it like, this cave? Was anything inside it?"

"Why, it was dark at first, but it was a place of power. Zorn said that of it. He did not want to go in, but I—" She bit her lip at the memory. "He was very much afraid, I think. Yet he said a binding spell against the fire. He set himself against it, and after a while ..."

Though she was telling the tale to Angborn, it was her brother she looked at now. "The fire could not stand against him," Llyndreth said proudly. "After a while, he triumphed."

"There was a fire in the cave?" urged Angborn. "What else? Where is it? Can you take me there?"

Llyndreth looked at him in surprise. "Why, Angborn?"

"My people left the arm ring behind. But they themselves vanished. I have never known what happened. But perhaps ... if the arm ring takes its power from the cave, perhaps the truth lies there. Could you find this cave again, Sun's Daughter?"

"I think ... yes, I think that I could find it. But, Angborn, please don't ask that of me now! Not when Zorn ... afterward, yes. But not now ..."

The giant still knelt. "Long lifetimes ago," he said, with only a touch of bitterness, "I came to this mountain seeking answers. Then the Danturi turned me away. Now again it is a Danturin who balks me." He rose, sighing. "Very well. Throughout the years I have at least learned patience. I can wait until you have found your Danturin."

Llyndreth touched his arm. "I was trying to tell you, Angborn, I have learned to think of the cave whenever I wear the arm ring. It glows with power then, I feel the power, too, inside me. It shuts out all things else. Even—even Zorn."

178

Her eyes fell. "I had to shut that out. I could not help him, feeling what the arm ring told me. I could not act at all."

She looked up at the Eodan pleadingly. "Help me once more, Angborn, and then Zorn and I together will help you. You shall have your answers if the arm ring can give them. It shall serve all three of us."

"Llyndreth!" The lord Rothwyn was begging, too. "I swore to our father that I would protect you. Forget this madness and come home."

Angborn turned hard eyes on him. "Madness? Yours was the madness when you set out to slay Danturi. Was it not enough that your forefathers had stolen the forests and valleys from them? No, you must take the mountain, too.

"It was in your footsteps that your sister followed. In those footsteps she has found her fate, and she cannot turn back. Nor can I. My fate waits here also.

"But you, Lord Rothwyn. Neither the mountain nor the arm ring holds aught for you. Do you go home to your soldiers' widows and the ashes of your castle. That is where your destiny lies."

Pale and silent, Rothwyn stood holding his war steed's reins. Almost, it seemed that he would mount and ride away. Then he raised his head and faced old Angborn. There was no longer any pleading in his eyes.

"You mistake, Eodan," he said quietly. "I, too, have found my fate upon the mountain. It was to fail and find myself a fool and see the ghost lights of my dead in every dark I come to. That, and to serve my sister. I have no other destiny, here or elsewhere."

With a little cry, Llyndreth was at her brother's side. They did not speak, but in the darkness her hand found his. "Rest now, sister," he said finally, "and wait for daybreak. Tomorrow you shall lead us where you will."

"It's there," Rothwyn said, pointing. "Right up there where you were hidden in the cave. You came stumbling down the slope. I couldn't forget, not ever."

Llyndreth looked up, shuddering a little. She herself remembered the long, fearful loneliness and what came after.

"Here is the plan," said Rothwyn. "You'll go there, just as before. Only this time Angborn will go with you. Me, I'll hide the horses. Then I'll scout about and try to find the priest-cave you spoke of."

"No! Let's stay together, Rothwyn."

"Not likely, I've thought this all out. It's the best way, Llyndreth."

"It's a terrible way. I won't wait in the cave knowing you're in danger. You didn't even want to come."

"I wanted to come. Else I wouldn't be here. No one forced me, did they?

"Furthermore, I'm still your elder brother. And your liege lord, kindly remember. You're supposed to show me some respect." Rothwyn grinned, a trifle sourly. "You stayed in the cave when Zorn bade you. Why can't you do the same for me?"

"That's just it," Llyndreth whispered. "Zorn never came back."

"Well, I shall. It's broad daylight. There won't be goblins swarming all over the mountain looking for me. They'll all be sleeping. And I won't have your pony with me, as Zorn did. Besides—" Rothwyn stopped. He'd been about to say he thought Zorn had let himself be followed. But it was as well, maybe, not to mention that.

"Tell her it's a good plan, Eodan," he said instead. "I might have known she wouldn't listen to her brother."

"It is best we go to the cave," said Angborn slowly. "If the Danturi have one chance of finding your brother, they have thrice that of catching the lot of us."

"It's all settled then," Rothwyn said cheerily. "You might argue with me but not with Angborn's logic."

But Llyndreth clung to him until he broke away. "Take care, Rothwyn. And hurry back before sunset. If you had worn the arm ring, as I have, you would know how much there is to dread."

There had been time, she was sure, for a dozen suns to set. If it was to be as before ... if Rothwyn, too, was to suffer on her account ...

"It has been overlong," she whispered to Angborn.

"It has been less than the flicker of an Eodan eyelash. You should learn patience. There has not been a Solgant ever born—no, not one—who knew the meaning of patience."

Angborn was peering through the hole that led to the priest-cave. "So through here," he muttered, "is the Danturin priest-place. And beyond that, the slab.

"If you would but lend me the arm ring, I could squirm through and see how it glows near the door. No farther than that, I swear it. I'd be gone moments only—"

"Angborn, you promised."

"Ah, well." Angborn sighed. "I did promise. But it's hard to be so close and do nothing. If I did not have the patience of pure stone, I would be tempted."

Hard also, thought Llyndreth, to sit still in this place and not think of Zorn. Of Zorn and Rothwyn, Rothwyn and Zorn. If Rothwyn too should fall—

Then, without warning, there was a scraping of boots against rock as her brother clambered into the cave.

"It is past sunset," Llyndreth accused. "You broke your word."

"Well, I cracked it a little, at the least." Rothwyn settled himself comfortably against the wall of the cave. "But not for the joy of it, I promise you. It's not my notion of sport at all, being alone in the dark when you know your enemies can see things that you can't and sniff out whatever they can't see.

"There was a goblin passed within touching distance of me where I lay, not once but twice. An old one, I'd wager, judging from the way he walked. And a good thing for me that he was old, too. Your ordinary sharp-nosed, keen-eyed goblin would've had me in no time.

"However—" Rothwyn sat up triumphantly. "However, it was worth it. The old fellow visited your warrior cave—was that what Zorn called the place? And on his way back, I followed him.

"I think—am almost sure of it, in fact—that I've found the way to your Halls of Darkness."

Llyndreth leaped to her feet.

"Gently, Sister. Gently. There's a difficulty. Besides the insanity of entering at all, I mean.

"It's dark inside that corridor. As dark as a world of goblins could want it. And what I want to know is, how are we to travel through it without a light?"

"There's the arm ring," said Llyndreth. "I could make it glow."

"And shine a signal of our coming to all goblindom? I think not." he paused. "Of course, if one of us had night eyes . . ."

"No," said Angborn flatly. "Oh, no. I can guess what you are thinking, Solgant. You are thinking I should turn fox or bat or some such and lead you down inside the earth. Well, I'll not do it. I can tell you that."

"*Will* not?" Llyndreth echoed in surprised. "Is it a case of will not? I thought you could not change shape but only size."

"It's a very strong word, *cannot*," said the Eodan, sounding uncomfortable. "Perhaps too strong a word. *Can* scarcely comes closer to the mark. If things were desperate enough—"

"But they are desperate! They are! There's Zorn. And after Zorn, we've your people to find out about. Oh, Angborn, the sooner I can reach King Myrgg . . . do, please, lead us to him.

"Only not as a bat. Back home in the loft once a bat flew straight at me. Bats are awful creatures!"

"They're quite harmless animals, most of them," Angborn grumbled. "You are a silly girl to dread them. And I am the fool of the world if I change shape on your account. If I go on four legs, you'll be tromping on top of me in the darkness. And I've told your brother already how it is, shaping myself into a bird. If you'd ever tried it, you would know how miserable it is afterward, getting your feet back on the ground.

"A night bird would be even worse. I'd be stumbling half-blind through the daylight like your Danturin friend for days piled on days."

"But Angborn—"

"*But Angborn*," the giant repeated acidly. "Oh, I know how it will be. You will coax and coax, and in the end I shall find myself an owl, flapping into some unchancy hole that reeks of goblins. It is the price one pays for being patient."

Suddenly his voice held a hint of laughter. "We shall see how desperate things are. If I'm to play owl for you, someone must carry my Old Spinner. Are we so desperate as that, Sun's Daughter?"

Llyndreth shrank back against her brother. "Never mind," said Rothwyn. Whatever thing his 'Old Spinner' is, I shall carry it for him."

"That you shall not. Do you think I'd trust my velvet-legged pet to a great, blundering Solgant warrior? It is your sister or no one.

"How shall it be, Llyndreth? You must let her walk up your arm so that she knows to trust you. And she must nestle in your cloak, close up by your heart as she does mine, for the warmth and safety of it."

There was silence in the cave for a long moment. Then, with a shuddering sigh, the girl held out her arm.

"Let you find your night eyes and your feathers, Angborn. If I'm to face goblins before the night is out, I'd as well begin with spiders!"

When last she had braved the darkness inside the mountain, Zorn himself had led her. Now it was Rothwyn she walked beside. Llyndreth took small comfort from his presence. Her brother was as much afraid as she, though he whispered most lightheartedly. His arm was a shade too stiff around her shoulders, his jokes a shade too merry for real mirth.

She must not think of Zorn nor of what the arm ring had let her feel. She must think only that soon, very soon now, she would face the Danturin king. She would need to be brave then, even braver than her father had been, and very strong.

The owl fluttered back and settled on her shoulders. "All clear," he rumbled. "How does my Spinner? Does she ride comfortably inside your cloak?"

"Safe against my breastbone." If she sounded peevish, it was no more than she felt. The spider was, in fact, clinging quite motionless inside warm folds of cloth. It was Llyndreth's arms, neck, and shoulders that crawled, still quivering in rebellion against the touch of eight excessively spiderlike feet.

Why could not Angborn had let Rothwyn carry his wretched pet?

At once Llyndreth felt ungrateful. She was asking much more than this of her Eodan friend. He had changed shape for her. He was waiting still—after long, long ages of waiting—to find out about his people.

And if she could not be brave enough to carry a single, harmless spider . . .

The owl's claws settled gently on her shoulder. "Curve up ahead." That was another thing that bothered her. It was hard to make herself believe the bird was Angborn. His voice was wrong, too hoarse and mournful.

She was not meant to deal with magic. She had not been born to it.

She was thinking that when she stumbled and went down. Angborn had warned her of the curve but not of the uneven ground beneath her feet. Birds, she remembered, biting her lips against the tears, did not concern themselves with what was underfoot.

Rothwyn hauled her to her feet. "Are you all right?"

"Yes."

Well, she was all right. Outside of having scraped half the skin from her right knee. It stung wickedly. Before long, probably, the knee would stiffen on her. But she must be ready to stand far worse if she were to succeed in her plan.

She could endure the pain better than the helpless blindness. The arm ring she carried was a sore temptation. She had but to clasp it on and think hard, very hard, of the cave's power. She would then have light enough to see by.

Enough to warn the Danturi.

Llyndreth stumbled on without a light.

Blackness and stone. Stone and blackness. Did it go on forever, then? The blackness seemed thick enough to touch. Yet it had no substance; the stones stabbed through to trip you, to rip your flesh, and still there was the blackness.

Somewhere it must end. Somewhere ahead lay King Myrgg's realm. And Zorn, paying out the price for helping her. And her fate that Angborn spoke of—

Then the owl was back, swooping down suddenly this time, not stopping to light on her shoulder. "Danturi ahead," he cried. "Two of 'em."

She must not panic. For only a moment. Llyndreth hesitated. Then she shook off Rothwyn's arm and began to run.

She no longer heeded the risk of falling. She fumbled with the arm ring as she ran, got it somehow around her arm. Somehow, moving all the while, she fastened the catch.

And now, she opened her whole mind to the cave of fire. To live flame dancing through the great portals. To banked embers aglow like gemstones in the wall. To the greater power still sleeping in the darkness. Let it awake, that power.

The arm ring was that power. It glowed pale green first, then blue—the heart of fire. Then it shone white-hot silver.

She herself was the power. A hungry, eager light, devouring darkness. She streamed through the black halls.

Then she was on the Danturi. She lifted her arm a little so that the light shone full in their faces. She knew what that would do, what it would have done to Zorn.

It did not fail. Their shadows jerked horribly like the nightmare goblins of her dreams. She saw their shocked faces, like Zorn's and yet unlike. Then they fell backward, throwing up their hands against the pain.

And still she was running.

Her mind was empty; the arm ring, dull and lifeless. Behind her, she heard dim sounds of scuffling. They had nothing to do with her. One thing only had meaning: to reach the end of her quest.

She was winded now, her hand tight against a stitch in her side. But up ahead was—she would not have called it light, once. Even now by any Solgant standards it was darkness. But it was the dark of a moonlit night, a dark you could see shape in, and movement.

There was sound in it, also. The humming sound of a many-voiced city.

Llyndreth crouched, panting, and looked her first on the Danturin Halls of Darkness.

ZORN STOOD, HIS WRISTS KNOTTED BEHIND HIM, AND STARED DOWN at the great stone slab that raised King Myrgg's throne above the floor. Little need, he thought, of binding his wrists. There was no way out of the hall save its heavily guarded entrance tunnel, nor had he the strength to escape if there had been a thousand open doors.

Gryth had come close enough, after all, to getting his wish; his spear, as it drove into Zorn's side, had smashed two ribs, leaving behind a great, deep gash that had nearly bled him dry. Untended, he would surely have died. But the Shadow Warriors had brought him home—as if he still had a home —to the Warrior Compound and had nursed him as tenderly as the greatest hero. Someone, though it was never Gryth, had been ever present to tend him in his helplessness.

He was whole now. Whole enough, at least, to stand upright before the Shadow King and his Warriors and be judged a traitor. It would not matter, afterward, that his ribs were still tightly bound and that a very little exertion left him aching and weak-legged.

It was not only stone walls that encircled him. Looking grimly down at his bowed head was King Myrgg, to whom he was oath-broken. And ringed all around him were those who had been his spear brothers and hearth friends. No need of looking to picture their impassive faces. Not even Guroc's would hold anything just now. To show anger or triumph or—unlikely as it surely was—sympathy for the prisoner would be unseemly; it would lower the dignity of the Danturin Council.

"Prisoner," said King Myrgg, "have you aught to say in your defense?"

Zorn raised his eyes and gave Myrgg the honor of his full title. "Na, Lord of the Shadows, Ruler of the Mountain, King and Kingmaker of the Danturi. Nothing."

The voice sounded dry and brittle in his ears, but he was managing to keep his own face empty. It was not so difficult. Perhaps it was because he was still weak that he felt so little. Or, perhaps, having long since found himself guilty, he could not care overmuch who else condemned him.

"Is there one among us who will speak for the accused?" There would be no one, as King Myrgg well knew. But there could be no justice without the chance of a defense.

Zorn's palms were sweating a little. Not from fear. The time for fear was past. But he could not forget those two empty seats in the Council ring, the space not yet filled where Gurd and Eloch should be sitting. And he could feel Gryth's presence.

Beyond the throne lay another, much smaller but more sacred chamber. You could smell the smoke from it now. Hrald the Old was making a mighty to-do about getting the fire ready. Well, it was a great day in his life, most likely. He had never been called on before to cast the Spell of Judgment on a traitor. Not he nor any archpriest of living memory—

"He who breaks faith with his people," King Myrgg was saying, "injures not us alone. His fault lies heavy on those who follow after and on those who have gone before. And each offense carries its proper vengeance. Should you find the prisoner guilty, you of the Warrior Council shall deal with the here and now. It is for the priest-kind to punish the rest."

There was an uneasy shuffling of feet. Brave as the Shadow Warriors were, none relished such close contact with Priest-Bane. And the knowledge of it was drifting even now into the Council chamber on the wings of old Hrald's smoke. The pungent, sweetish smell was making Zorn a little sick. Someone choked back a cough.

Even King Myrgg spoke a little more hurriedly as though he too were eager to be finished with the business. "At the prisoner's feet lies his breast piece; it is the mark of a Shadow Warrior. Let those of you who find for his innocence pass it by in peace. Those who find him guilty, let you thrust in your spears."

Shaft after shaft hummed close to Zorn's ankles until the leather between them bristled with spears. It was no more than he had expected. Next, he supposed, they would destroy his own ritual spear, the one he had carried to Council. His throat tightened. He and Gryth had spent long hours working on that spear.

The smashing seemed to take forever. Though the shaft was long since splintered, each warrior in turn must set his foot on it. But it was Hrald the priest's shrill voice that took most of Zorn's attention. The old man was chanting now, his cracked voice rising in an unending, tuneless mutter. And the smoke was dizzyingly thick and sweet.

Guroc's voice cut through the fog in Zorn's brain. "He is no true Danturin. It is not fitting that he should look like one. Let you give order, Mighty Myrgg, to crop his ears. Let him wear the mark of traitor where all can see."

The Council had grown very quiet. Zorn could hear the sound of his own ragged breathing. He had known he would face dishonor, but he had never thought of mutilation. Try as he might, he could not keep his eyes from Gryth's face. For a moment dismay seemed to flicker there. But doubtless his own wish had fooled him, for Gryth now looked hard and quite unmoved.

Very well. He could stand the pain if that were the required vengeance. It was not the thought of pain that twisted wickedly in his stomach but the shame of it. *Why could he not have died of Gryth's spear thrust?*

"Na, Guroc," said King Myrgg quietly. "For that the prisoner once saved the life of my sister-son, we will not crop his ears. Yet we will set the mark of traitor on him. Even as we have stripped him of his shield and spear, we shall strip the hair from his face. Let him go bald-skinned like his friends the Solgants.

"And this is the King's judgment on him, that he shall be brought forth on Feast and Council and Market days that the Danturi may look on him, all to scorn the face of a traitor."

Mercy? wondered Zorn heavily. Did Myrgg truly think he had given mercy? If they had but cropped his ears as Guroc demanded and left him to live out his doom alone in some dark, peaceful place . . .

His face was raw from the scraping of warriors' hunting knives and bleeding in a half-dozen places from careless nicks.

"Let you be swift, Lorki," said the king, glancing uneasily toward the smoke-filled inner chamber. "The priest-kind are waiting. He is theirs once you have done and taboo afterward to all ordinary folk."

The last and least of the Shadow Warriors gave a nervous swipe at an imaginary patch of fur and drew blood from Zorn's chin. What need has he to be so jumpy, Zorn wondered irritably. He is under no Priest-Bane. But he knew that in Lorki's place, he would have been just as eager to be finished.

For a little, he had been so sick inside at the thought of public shame that he had half forgotten the judgment yet before him. Now a fresh dread grew in him as he watched the warriors drawing back, little by little. Already, they felt the taboo. They would not come close to him again. No closer, at least, than spitting distance . . .

Fear flickered in the warriors' eyes and warned him. Turning, he saw the three hooded figures emerging from the smoky darkness. On either side walked the torchbearers. Slowly. Somberly. But in the middle, Hrald the Old was dancing. It was a stiff, awkward dance as if his bones were strung together with uneven leather thongs, but there was a wildness in it. The triumph of a traitor taken.

By torchlight Hrald's shadow danced too. It stretched and shrank as the flames flickered, and against the cave walls the tiny knife he held loomed long and sharp.

Zorn was sweating. He could keep his face stiff, but there was nothing he could do about the sweat. With his hands bound, he cold not even wipe it away. It was unfair that his own body should rob him of what painfully small dignity he had left.

And then the dancing stopped. Hrald was chanting again, his face and arms uplifted to the ceiling of the cave. His old man's voice was so brittle and cracked that Zorn could make out only a little. He tried to remember the words from his childhood, but he had not paid much attention. A curse against traitors had meant little to him, for he had been passionately loyal to King Myrgg and had adored each Shadow Warrior as a mighty hero. He had never imagined his worst enemy capable of treachery, let alone himself. And now—

Hrald was saying something about the sun. "Till the sun kneels weeping in the halls of darkness." Which meant never, Zorn supposed. But it reminded him briefly of Llyndreth. He hoped she had gotten clear of the mountain. Hoped she had found the arm ring, too. Would she weep for him? he wondered.

Then he forgot about Llyndreth. For the torchbearers had

set their lights in hollowed-out stone pockets and were baring his chest, leading him toward Hrald.

He could scarcely see the old priest's gray-furred, shrunken face. But cold, merciless eyes glared at him from inside the hood. And the odor of the purification fires was strong in his nostrils.

This time the words were clear. Agonizingly clear.

"He who betrays his people, he who sheds his spear brother's blood, he who breaks taboo—"

Hrald plunged the knife in just below Zorn's breastbone. But not far. It was a tiny knife, after all, despite the looming shadow, and it made only a prick. It hurt less, Zorn thought with surprise, than the nicks on his cheekbone and jaw.

"—he shall suffer the Living Death. His blood shall turn to fire; his bones, to ice. Long shall he wither. And yet not die."

Only a prick, Zorn told himself. And no pain to speak of. But Hrald's amber eyes gleaming at him were the eyes of an old wolf. Na, the eyes of long-dead Dantur claiming his vengeance.

Long shall he wither—the chamber wavered dizzily with sweet, thick, choking smoke—*and yet not die.*

20

KING MYRGG'S PALACE. A CURIOUS NAME FOR A KING, AND A CURI-
ous place he held his court in. Llyndreth had pictured Solgant
castles—she knew now how foolish her fancy had been. This
was nothing like.

It was, instead, a great open court, if a place enclosed by
rock might be called open. There were no walls—none, at
least, that she could see—save those formed by the mountain.

And it was filled with people. Or with dim shapes, rather,
whose large amber eyes seemed almost to move of themselves, independent of any bodies. Coldly hostile eyes staring
at you, through you, beyond you from every possible direction.

Llyndreth shrank back, telling herself all the while that no
one was really staring at her. Had she been noticed, someone
would have given warning.

Moreover, somewhere within that wilderness of gleaming,
shifting, disembodied eyes was the Danturin king she had

come to find. And mayhap Zorn. She must move amid it to find out.

Yet to those eyes, she was no vague and shadowy shape. If they but looked, the Danturi could see her as plainly as they saw each other. Llyndreth gazed ruefully at her arm ring. If this were a made-up story, such as she and Marnne had once told each other, the metal band would turn her invisible. How handy that would be!

But such a wish was unworthy. Already the Eodan and the arm ring together had done more magic for her than she had once dreamed might exist.

And Zorn. In the cave of fire he had stood fast against a strange and fearsome power and had not faltered. Could she not do the same?

Presently the pattern of things grew a trifle clearer and less terrifying. The shapes moved in groups to and from little booths along the stone walls. There were a few small, wispy torches set high and far back, and she could make out smoke rising from various of the booths. Torches and cook fires, as she supposed these last to be, gave off a faint, murky light.

There were walkways also. It was none so different from Market day at home, she thought with surprise. Not if you set aside the fact that these were goblins. No one was expecting an outworlder. All the barterers were busy with their own affairs. Perhaps no one would notice....

Timidly, drawing her cloak close about her as if that could somehow make a difference, Llyndreth stepped at last into the throng. She picked her way carefully at first, dreading lest she bump headlong into a Danturin. But no one else was poking about so. She tried to move more boldly, to pretend that she belonged.

She had moved a good way through the crowd now and could see that at the end of the court farthest from where she had begun—she might have known it would be farthest!—stone steps rose upward. There were stone portals, too, not at all like those in the cave of fire, but most assuredly man-made. These, she supposed, marked the king-place of the Danturi. She worked her way toward them as best she could, trying to move as part of the crowd and yet to avoid meeting those fearsome goblin eyes.

One step more, Llyndreth told herself. And then another. She had had more luck already than one might dare to hope for.

And then the thing she had dreaded happened. A Danturin woman brushed against her, turned—mayhap to ask her pardon—and looked full in her eyes. She had thought the Danturi would fall on her at once when first she was seen for what she was. They were goblins, after all—fierce warrior creatures. It did not happen so.

The woman stepped back, wide-eyed, almost stumbling in her haste. She opened her mouth to speak and failed and tried again.

Llyndreth walked on. Hurrying a little, she wedged her way into the heart of the crowd. Closer and closer to the king's high throne. Each step a tiny triumph.

Above, the king loomed dimly, his warriors ranged round him on either side. Zorn would have sat there once. Where was he this night?

Now the woman who had seen her was making noise enough, and not that woman only. From neighbor to neighbor, the word spread through the hall. *Solgant,* ran the murmur. *Outworlder. An outworlder among us.* It was half a wail, as it spread from tongue to tongue, and half an outraged growl. Llyndreth shivered at the sound of it.

It had reached the king's dais, for the warriors were standing, one by one. They had their spears out, some of them. They were no threat, not yet, for there was too much confusion in the court below. They had not spotted her.

But soon. Very soon. The Danturi had their eyes full open now. They glanced at one another suspiciously. There were eyes on Llyndreth once more, fierce amber goblin eyes ringing her around. Yet those nearest made no move to take her prisoner. They moved back, instead, leaving her in the open —prey to the Shadow Warriors' spears.

It was then that she saw Zorn. Not bound. There was no need to bind him. He half sat, half lay, leaning against the base of the king's dais as though he needed its support. His face was scraped raw as she had seen it in the vision. He was ragged and very dirty.

Before him stood a Danturin woman and a boy not yet near manhood. The woman gave something to her son. At a word from her, he let fly a small handful of gravel.

Not stones alone, but shame also, thought Llyndreth, flinching inwardly at the sight. It was more than the prisoner did. He stared blankly ahead as though he felt nothing, as though a tiny trickle of blood were not running down his cheek.

He had been proud, so proud. Too arrogant to take water when he was feverish and thirsting. "I am Zorn, Captain of Shadow Warriors," he had said.

Now he was Zorn the traitor and must endure such scorn as this. She had done this to him. She and the king he had been proud to serve and the spear brothers he had boasted of.

Llyndreth was angry, suddenly, far too angry to be afraid. She glared up at the Shadow Warriors. Let them dare to cast a spear at her before she had had her say! She willed them not to.

Let them look their fill at her, these goblins. They would hear from her soon enough. Her chin jutting forward, battle-ready, Llyndreth marched boldly toward the foot of the steps.

She knelt on the bottom step but kept her head very high. "King of the Danturi," she said quite loudly, "I have come to beg a boon."

Zorn heard the murmurs echoing through the chamber, but he paid them little mind. Sometimes, he had learned, he could go away from himself, shutting out present ugliness and pain by setting his mind very firmly on some pleasanter time from the past.

The sudden silence roused him. It was seldom quiet on a Court-and-Market Day, never silent. Then he heard the voice. A young, clear female voice that gave a strange Solgant quirk to long-familiar words. There was one person only who used the Common Speech with such an accent.

Painfully, Zorn twisted himself about for a better view of the steps to his left. It was Llyndreth, truly. Llyndreth the Sun-Born, whom he had never thought to see again.

She was kneeling to Myrgg. Or pretending to kneel, perhaps; for she was spear-shaft straight from the waist up, like a young queen, and Zorn felt a thrill of pride in her.

In that moment, he could not think at all but only watch, unbelieving, hungry for the sight of her.

Pride, then stinging shame. He scrubbed futilely at the smear of blood drying along his cheek. Not spittle, this time, but blood, yet a mark of dishonor for all that. It was dark here in Myrgg's court. If there was any good fortune left him in the world, she had not seen what had happened. If it were only dark enough to blind her Solgant eyes, she might not see him at all—

"—to plead," she was saying, "for your warrior Zorn, whom you have named a traitor." So she had seen. Had seen him helpless, humbled. Zorn's thoughts whirled crazily. She was no prisoner. Had she come then of her own free will? She who feared bats and crawling things and goblins, she who so feared the dark. Was she alone?

The danger of it struck him like a great, sickening blow in the belly. Never before had a Solgant entered the Realm below the Mountain. The Danturi would think her a spy, a trespasser at best. Mayhap the priest-kind would think her presence a profanation. They would never let her go alive. And he was powerless to help her.

"He did not betray you," Llyndreth was saying passionately. "He never meant to harm his people. But he owed me his life, or thought he did, at least, so he would not let your warriors take me prisoner. The Danturi do not break their debts, he said. And because he was Danturin, he would not leave his own unpaid."

"But yet," said King Myrgg, "he betrayed a greater trust. He set his hand against his spear brothers. Never again will Gurd cast a spear because of him. And Eloch near died."

Zorn relaxed a little. The king was giving ear to her. Even showing her courtesy. It could not help him, of course. Nothing she might say could help a foredoomed traitor. But Myrgg prized courage above all else. Llyndreth's boldness might save her, at least.

"It was because of me," Llyndreth insisted. "The fault was mine, not his. Whatever bane it is you have laid on Zorn, let him go free. Let it fall on me instead."

She was weeping now, not even trying to hide it. Never before had Zorn seen her cry.

The court spun round him in a dizzy blur as he pushed to his elbow. It was madness, pure and simple, her asking to suffer in his place. She did not understand about the Living Death. The king would not grant that, could not. Yet if she talked on, Myrgg might decide to punish her too.

Somehow, though Zorn had been very sure he was past helping anyone, he must prevent that.

With effort, Zorn made it to his feet. He was not sure his legs would hold him, but somewhere—somewhere—he must find the strength. Uncertainly, he stumbled toward King Myrgg's throne.

"It may not be," he said in the strongest voice he could muster. "It is for the Danturi only. You know that, my liege. You know it is a doom for traitors only, and she is Solgant and no traitor. They cannot punish Solgants, the priest-kind can't. And the Council can't either."

He was running out of breath, not sure he was even making sense. His legs were wretchedly wobbly, and behind him, very vaguely, he could hear Guroc insisting that the Solgant woman was most certainly a spy and, as such, ought to be put to death. He longed to put his hands around Guroc's throat. But it had been a long time now since he had had the power for that.

At any rate, it was not Guroc who mattered. It was King Myrgg and perhaps Hrald High Priest, too. He focused unsteadily on the king.

"Let one of us march boldly into a Solgant court," complained Guroc in his most self-important tone, "and well you know what thing would happen. Besides, she knows now where lies our stronghold."

He must answer that, Zorn thought desperately, and he was not sure how. If only his head would stop whirling—

But then Gryth spoke. "If the Solgant woman will promise silence, I myself will take her from the mountain. And also I will stand surety for her faith. I think she did not come to spy."

"She came," said Guroc angrily, "in league with a traitor."

Then Gryth rose from his place at the king's right hand. He moved lazily, without haste, but his golden eyes glinted. "I tire of your venom, Guroc," he said. "Let you be silent this once."

"I ask the king's heir's pardon. Does he bear so much love, then, to Solgants and traitors?"

"Sa, Guroc," Gryth said in his gentle drawl. "Mayhap there be Solgants and traitors both who deserve it more than you."

There was a flurry of shocked whispers that died as Gryth went on. "This long time have I watched you shame the fallen. And I tried to join in your scorn. But all the while, I have known that Zorn was more man and warrior than you. Even on the day he broke our trust, I knew it. When he lay with my spear in his side and I spat on him, crying out that I was glad of his wound, I knew it then also."

Gryth turned his eyes on Zorn. "Let you know I lied in saying I was glad. In my heart I wept for my spear brother."

He looked with open approval on Llyndreth. "I know this day why he betrayed my trust. It was a bold thing to come here, lady. It does you honor."

Guroc was protesting. "My liege. My liege. Do not let him dishonor me so. He cannot claim that I am less than a traitor!"

"Silence!" Myrgg roared the word. "I'll not have my Shadow Warriors at one another's throats like starving wolves. And in my own court, too!"

But at that moment gnarled old fingers grasped the king's shoulder. Hrald the Old had crept forth from his his high seat behind the throne. "Lord of the Shadows," he said, his voice shrill and trembling, "did you note it? She begged for the Living Death. And she knelt weeping."

Myrgg clung hard to his temper. He was still quite angry with Gryth and Guroc. Let them try being king for a while, and they would find that it had plenty of problems without their tugging at him like wolf cubs over a disputed bone. Whatever he did now with that wretched Solgant woman, it was sure to be wrong. If he let her go free, Guroc would say he was too easy. If he punished her, Gryth would sulk. Myrgg was very fond of his sister's son. Once he had been fond of Zorn too. . . .

Well, he must humor Hrald. One was not lightly rude to a high priest, not even when one was king. "I suppose she wept," he muttered. "What of it?"

"What of it?" Hrald's voice had been high before. Now he was shrieking. It made Myrgg's head ache.

Hrald bobbed up and down, his head wobbling from side to side within his hood. "Myrgg, Myrgg, Myrgg," he wailed. "You never were a scholar.

"You're a fine war leader and a good enough king when it comes to settling disputes. But you went to sleep whenever I sang our history, and as for the spells you ought to know, a snail knows more magic than you."

"I did not sleep." growled King Myrgg. It was not right that Hrald should shame him before his warriors. It was not improving his temper any.

"You slept!" accused the old priest. "And you're sleeping now. Do you not remember any of the Destiny?"

Myrgg squirmed. "Well—"

"Let you listen, then. And try not to sleep this time."

"To the children of Dantur, the Mountain.
Theirs to hold
Till the Sun kneels weeping in the Halls of Darkness."

The old priest paused. "Do you see? Do you?"

"Oh, I say," said Myrgg. "I always thought that was just a fancy kind of priest talk for saying 'never.' The sun can't kneel. The real sun, I mean.

"Of course"—he glanced uneasily at Llyndreth—"if it means one of the Sun-Born—"

"That's not all," said Hrald. His voice dropped in pitch. There was an ominous note to his chanting.

"Theirs to hold
Till the Three Races stand as one
To seek the Living Death."

Myrgg swallowed hard. "Well," he said. "She did ask for it after a fashion. But not by name. And she's only one Solgant. That lacks a lot of being 'Three Races.'"

"Fool," Hrald hissed. "There was Zorn, our own traitor. He claimed it as his own. A son of Dantur makes two. There lacks only the Eodan."

"Eodan?"

"You've forgotten the Eodans?" Hrald was near weeping.

206

"The Old Ones? Those who held the mountain before us? It was they who made the Destiny!"

A note of sarcasm crept into his voice. "You do remember Dantur's brother, my lord Myrgg? He who betrayed us and must even now be nameless?"

"Certainly!" Myrgg snapped. "Most certainly I remember. Sold us out to the Solgants. Cost us the great battle for the outworld, the one where Dantur took his death wound.

"It's where the Living Death comes from. Dantur cursed him with it before he died—his brother and all traitors afterward."

"And you remember how he betrayed us? What messenger he sent to warn the Solgants?"

Myrgg glared. A fine time it was that old Hrald had picked to quiz him on history! Was it not enough that he had Solgants to deal with at the moment, and traitors, and warriors who quarreled among themselves? By Hrald's way of it, the mountain would soon be falling on top of him too. "An outworlder, I suppose," he growled. "No Danturin could have done it."

"An outworlder, yes! An Eodan. With Dantur's greatest treasure, the traitor bribed an Eodan. Yet the Old Ones stood our friends in those days, no enemy to anyone.

"And when it was known what had come to pass, Eldeon —who was the first and greatest among the Eodans—passed judgment on his people. Since one among them had helped the Solgants to drive us from our land, their mountain should be ours. For a time, Myrgg! For a time!

"And as for them, they should go home to the stones they

had sprung from. They should sleep amid the stones, their kin, till the awaking time. For the Eodans came to be even as the mountains were born. It is said they cannot die until the crumbling of the last rock—"

Zorn passed a hand wearily across his face. The king looked short-tempered. Small wonder if he was. Zorn himself could not keep track of the high priest's tale. Almost, for a little, he had forgotten his own pain. But he ached sorely now, was shivering—*his bones shall turn to ice. . . .*

Only one thing seemed to matter now, that Llyndreth should get safe away. If the king would but give Gryth leave to take her. Myrgg might, perhaps, if old Hrald would end his gibbering.

A hand touched his arm. Llyndreth was not crying any more, though there were tear marks on her face. "They would not listen to me," she said. "But perhaps they will let me stay."

To have her with him— But he had been a stranger himself, for a time, in a strange and blinding land.

"Na," he said. "You would never see the sun again. In time, you would come to hate me."

She would have made a good warrior. She did not protest. She looked at him steadily, and there was nothing that he had ever dreaded in her face—not the shrinking back from a goblin, nor shame at his downfall, nor even pity. Only a fierce, warm, terrible pride.

"You left a thing on the hillside," she said, "that was given to you. I have brought it back again, more-than-friend."

Drawing the arm ring from beneath her cloak, she clasped it on him. Zorn did not notice the warmth of its power, nor was he aware when it began to glow. He saw only the pride in Llyndreth's eyes.

Slowly, the sound of the high priest's sobbing brought him back. Crouched at the foot of the king's throne, Hrald was staring down directly at him. The hood had fallen back, showing the sparse, faded fur atop Hrald's head and his thin, lizardlike neck, but the old man was paying no heed.

"It has come back," he cried hoarsely. "Dantur's arm ring, which was given to the Eodan so that he might betray us! The Sun has knelt weeping, and the Wanderer has returned. Two races have sought the Living Death, and the Eodan is sure to come. Then the Sleepers will awaken. No binding spell can hold them!

"Let us flee, Myrgg, flee. It is a day of doom for Dantur's children. Our reign beneath the mountain is ended!"

21

NUMBLY, ZORN GLANCED AT THE ARM RING, THEN AT THE STONE slab behind Myrgg's throne. The markings were the same! How blind he had been not to know at once. Hundreds of times he had knelt at the king's feet, looking directly toward the slab. Had seen it, yet not seen it.

He looked at old Hrald. He did not seem the same without his hood. No longer the awesome figure who had doomed him with a curse, the high priest seemed pitiful. A skinny, terrified old man.

Where could his people go, Zorn wondered, if Hrald were right? Had they beaten the Solgants back for nothing?

He did not understand any of this, had scarcely listened, at first, to what Hrald was saying. But one thing seemed clear. It was because of him that Llyndreth had come. To him that she had brought the arm ring.

Whatever happened next was somehow his own doing.

He touched the arm ring. It was glowing brightly. It was

a thing of power. He had learned that in the Cave of Fire. If he but knew how to use it . . .

He was puzzling over this, shutting his mind against the pain of the arm ring's brilliance, when a new uproar broke out in the back of the court.

You could say this much for the Solgant lord Rothwyn. He was not timid. He came into the hall storming, and it was all the two Danturin guards could do to hold him. They looked storm-tossed, all three of them, when it came to that. There had been a fight worth seeing somewhere in the corridor.

"What have you done with my sister?" he demanded, as though he were surrounded by his own troops and not a host of enemies. "If you've hurt her . . ."

Myrgg struggled for dignity. It is no easy task being kingly when your warriors have been bickering and your high priest is groveling at your feet, having just foretold the end of your reign.

He was not even angry at this last intrusion. It seemed a piece with all the rest of the night's work, having an enemy prisoner make demands as though he held you bound instead.

"We have done nothing to her. It was she who came, asking to take the place of the prisoner, Zorn."

"I knew she'd do that." Rothwyn sounded reproachful, as if the Danturi were somehow to blame for his sister's folly. "Well, you can't let her. If you need someone to punish, take me. I'm a better prize, by far, being her liege lord. And besides, it was I who brought an army onto your mountain."

He stopped for breath, and an owl settled onto his shoulder. "Or me," said the owl. "No doubt whatever doom it is requires patience. And I have acquired more patience in my day than all the Solgants and Danturi since the world began."

There was a moment of startled silence. Then Guroc stepped forward. "A talking owl," he said. "Never until these Solgants came into our hall did I ever hear a bird talk. It is some wicked Solgant spell making, surely. Let them be punished."

Hrald had buried his head in his arms. He lifted it now. "Na," he said gloomily, "it is the Eodan come to fulfill the Destiny. They were ever shape changers. It is complete now. We are done."

"Silence!" It was the second time this night King Myrgg had roared for silence. If this was indeed the last hour of his reign, he meant that it should be a peaceful one.

In the quiet that followed, you could hear it plainly beyond the great stone slab. It was the sound of rocks moving about, if it were that rocks could stir. The sound of slow footsteps shod in stone.

"The Sleepers waken," said old Hrald in a hushed, hopeless whisper.

Zorn knew now how it was. All the Danturin priest-places, every one of them, opened into the Cave of Fire. They were sealed with slabs, and the priests stood guardian.

Had stood guardian.

That was over now. Hrald was broken, a feeble, desperate old man. The whole priest-kind was broken.

There was only the arm ring. It took its power from the cave —or had seemed to. And yet they said it had been Dantur's. If it had been a thing worth coveting, a thing some long-ago Eodan broke his faith for, it must have powers of its own.

It had opened the door in the Cave of Warrior Making and sealed it once again. He wore the arm ring now. He would have to try its strength once more.

He looked upward. Five steps up the dais to the king's throne. Only five. But he was very weary. His legs were shaking.

Mayhap he had a destiny of his own. It might have been for this that he had lost and lost again. As a Shadow Warrior, he had had much to live for. Now nothing.

Yet he could not have tried yesternight. Not before Llyndreth's coming. Not before Gryth had called him spear brother once more.

He gathered his strength and slowly, one step at a time, hauled himself up to the king-place. Past Hrald. Past Myrgg, uneasy on his throne. Past the warriors who had condemned him. Into the priest-place forbidden him by taboo.

Light glowed around the edges of the slab, as he had known it would. Voices murmuring, and he had known that too. The arm ring shone fire-white. His hand before his eyes did not suffice. No way to shield them, none at all. It would not have been an agony to Dantur, he thought vaguely. Dantur had been born an outworlder. He had not spent his whole life in darkness.

Zorn knelt. Partly because it seemed the thing to do amid such power. But partly because he doubted his legs would hold him.

He must change the binding spell. He could not hope to send back the Sleepers. What he might do, he was not sure. Make their coming easier, perhaps; less dreadful, somehow. It was his to bear the brunt of it, he did know that. Because, unwittingly, he had called them forth. Because he wore the arm ring.

"Dwellers in darkness, keepers of the cave—" He was whispering. No need to shout. They were awake now. They would hear him.

He raised his arm, touching metal against the slab. "— sleepers within the stone, nor dead nor living, come forth in peace. By Dantur's charm be bound, and bide you peaceful—"

The slab was yielding. There was brightness all around him, more brightness than a Danturin should have to endure. It blinded him. It consumed him till he became the brightness.

The light he had become spun into darkness: whirling light-into-darkness, dizzying, shattering, ending at last in peaceful blackness.

He awoke to Llyndreth. She should not have come, he thought fuzzily. She should have gone with Gryth to the out-world.... If Myrgg had given leave ... he could not quite remember....

Then Angborn loomed over him, larger than he remembered. But perhaps he had never seen old Angborn at his fullest size—

"It was a foolhardy thing you did," the Eodan was saying. "Foolhardy and lacking in patience. You grow rash as a Solgant. If you had but given the arm ring to me, I could have saved you a good deal of trouble."

Perhaps it was because he was still a little dizzy that Angborn seemed to have grown. But you could not tell about Eodans. He would have paid more attention to Angborn—old fuss-and-grumble Angborn—if he had once supposed him to be an Old One.

Where were the Old Ones?

"Youngling," said a deep, calm voice. "Son of my daughter—"

Angborn sprang up at once. "Eldeon," he said. "Grandsire. I serve you."

It was odd to hear Angborn called "youngling." Zorn twisted his head on Llyndreth's lap so that he could see the speaker.

The stone slab had not moved, he saw. It had simply melted away. Zorn shuddered. He had set himself to challenge that power.

Eldeon stood where the slab had been. And beyond him, still within the Cave of Fire, the other Sleepers. They were giants, truly. Angborn stood the least among them. And their features seemed carved of rock. Only in the eyes was there any softness.

"It has been a long sleep, daughter's son," said Eldeon slowly. It seemed a ponderous effort. Lips, jaws, tongue all moved with stiffness, as though speech was an art to be relearned with time. "We have waited long for the Three Races to learn peace. Has the time come that we may reclaim the mountain?"

Angborn stared at him with dismay. "Was it that you waited for—peace among the peoples?"

"What else? For that one among us had injured the Danturi, we lent them our mountain. They were as children, then, and also the Solgants. Quarrelsome children.

"But they are as one now, the Solgants and Danturi and you also. Else we would not have wakened. Is it not so?"

Angborn bowed his head. "They are quarrelsome still," he said, low-voiced, "divided by a wall of hatred. You have waked too early, grandsire."

He paused, then went on even more reluctantly. "And yet you have slept too long. The Solgants have multiplied like rays of their own sun. There is no room for the Danturi in their land. Nor for our kind either."

The Sleepers crowded nearer, moving stiffly, awkwardly. "All this while in vain?" one of them protested.

Eldeon's craggy brow seemed more deeply furrowed. "But we waked," he said in puzzlement. "Not till the Three Races stood as one were we to wake."

Angborn gestured toward Zorn and Llyndreth. "So they did. These two and her brother and I. Only we. It was enough to rouse you.

"As for the wall of hatred," he said thoughtfully, "mayhap you did not sleep in vain entirely. Mayhap there is a crack in the wall."

There was a great sadness in Eldeon's face, a sadness cast in stone. "We dare sleep no more," he said, "else we forget to waken. But we have come full circle. Should we lay claim to the mountain, the Danturi are homeless wanderers."

"It is our mountain!" cried a voice. "We sprang from it. It was sacred to us before the first Danturin walked the earth."

"Ours once," said Eldeon very gently, "ere you learned to crave an arm ring. And sacred, yes. But not so sacred as peace and justice. We are younger kin to rock and earth, elder kin of Danturi and Solgant. Let us not betray either kinship."

"We shall be wanderers ourselves."

"There are other mountains," said Eldeon.

"Not our mountain."

"Ours to claim," said Eldeon. "What foot of earth can be stranger to us when we know the rocks for kindred? The Danturi are younglings, blind and helpless for wandering. We are the Eodans, old as mountains, kindred to all things."

"We are the Eodans," murmured the Sleepers, "kindred to all things."

A woman stepped forward. She moved as though she had once been graceful. "Angborn," she said wonderingly.

Angborn knelt. "Lady mother," he said. She looked younger than he, untouched by all the ages she had slept. She was beautiful, a statue moving.

"Who challenged us," she asked, "bidding us to peace?"

Zorn struggled to find his voice, but it seemed to have dissolved with the stone slab. "He did," said Angborn. "The Danturin."

"There was pain in the bidding"—the lady looked down at Zorn—"and loneliness. It is a lonely business facing the unknown."

"So he has discovered," said Angborn dryly. "He befriended a Solgant, and his people named him traitor."

"Ah, then he has suffered! 'Long shall he wither,'" she repeated, "'and yet not die.' We had heard of Dantur's Bane before we slept.

"But you will be whole again." She touched Zorn's forehead with his fingertips. They were cold, cold as stone, but soft with returning life. "All that had been bound was unbound when we awakened."

Eldeon stood beside her. "You could be king, you know. King of the Danturi. When the priest-kind find that we have left the mountain—"

Zorn shook his head. He had never thought to be king. That was to Gryth when Myrgg should breathe his last. And besides, he had lain too long at the king's feet, despised, unwanted. He was not sure he could walk among the warriors ever again.

And there was Llyndreth, who had come to offer the unthinkable. Llyndreth, who was sitting with him now, almost timidly, as if none of this were her doing—

"Just as well," said Eldeon. "There will be those, you know, who still will call you traitor."

Angborn looked down at Zorn. "I shall be going with my people now. My little kingdom will be empty, my animals untended." He paused. "But you were a Shadow Warrior once. You can be one again if you so choose. They will have to let you now."

Had been. That was the truth of it. He had been a Shadow Warrior and had broken his oath to help Llyndreth. He had chosen once. He would not choose and break his choice and choose again.

"Na," he said, at last finding his voice. "A man cannot walk backward all his life."

Angborn laughed. "Not without many a stumble."

Eldeon broke in. "We cannot leave the mountain wearing our true shape. The kingdom of the Danturi would be in ruins." He looked at his grandson anxiously. "Can you transform yourself? To a bird, perhaps? Birds would be best. They are light and swift, and we can fly far on our way."

Angborn swallowed hard. "Naturally," he said to Eldeon. "Why, only just lately I disguised myself as an owl!"

He looked down at Zorn and Llyndreth. "If you're to inherit my little kingdom, Danturin, you'll have to take my Old Spinner, too. She'd not like living among Solgants." He smiled at Llyndreth to take the sting from his words. "Not even a Solgant who deals in magic."

The girl was fighting tears. "Oh, Angborn," she whispered, "I'm glad you've found your people. But it's dreadful to lose friends. Dreadful to think of never seeing you again."

"Why, there's the arm ring, isn't there? Like enough, the Danturin will lend it to you if you ask nicely." His eyes were tender. "Farewell, Daughter of the Sun."

He turned to Zorn. "And you—you'll have to learn a little patience. Remember, you're the crack in the wall.

"May fortune shield you"—Angborn grinned suddenly, wickedly—"goblin."

Behind them Eldeon was chanting softly. "Eodans, kindred to bird-kind, wearers of wings . . ."

Outside the priest-place there were sounds of scuffling. "What do I care for your taboos?" growled an unmistakably Solgant voice. "My sister went there. Let me go up, I say!"

Then there was a great, swift roaring of wings.

They were birds no longer when the riders saw them last. The three sat their horses and watched, Rothwyn on his war steed, the pony Etheryll carrying double. He who had been a Shadow Warrior sat the saddle; clinging behind him, Llyndreth the Sun-Born.

The Eodans did not look like giants from this distance. They were tiny, toiling specks far across the wasteland. Presently, the darkness took them so that Zorn alone could see.

"Sa," he said, turning the Solgant pony round. "Let us go home, Queen of Warriors."

91-92 $13.95

F
ZET   Zettner, Pat

The Shadow Warrior

NOV 1 2 [illegible]   JUN 0 1 2005

OCT 2 5 1999

APR 1 0 2000

MAY 0 9 [illegible]

OCT 1 8

MAY 14

FEB 1 2 2003

FEB 2 8 2003

MAR 0 1 2004

WASHINGTON MIDDLE SCHOOL LIBRARY
Olympia, Washington